Where the Deer
and the
Cantaloupe Play

Where the Deer and the Cantaloupe Play

A Novel by

T. Ernesto Bethancourt

Oak Tree Publications, Inc.
San Diego, California

First Edition
Manufactured in the United States of America

For information write to:
Oak Tree Publications, Inc.
P.O. Box 1012
La Jolla, California 92038

Library of Congress Cataloging in Publication Data

Bethancourt, T. Ernesto.
  Where the deer and the cantaloupe play.

  SUMMARY: Despite the fact that Latino and Black cowboys do not appear in books, films or electronic media, a city-born Latino youth searches for a hero in America's historical past.
  [1. Hispanic Americans—Fiction. 2. Cowboys—Fiction] I. Title.
PZ7.B46627Wh [Fic] 80-27110
ISBN 0-916392-69-4

1 2 3 4 5 6 7 8 9 84 83 82 81

For my father, who I never realized was a hero
until it was too late to tell him.
And for the real-life Tom O'Hanlon,
who knows who he is.

Preface

This book is about dreams and heroes; not handguns. Despite its western setting, you will find no horsemen galloping through the sagebrush. What you *will* find is a great deal about the dreams of a city-born Latino youth in search of a hero in America's historical past, when books, film, electronic media and even History texts have denied the indisputable fact that there were, indeed, Latino and black cowboys on both sides of the law.

The technical data, held to a minimum, represents two years of research. During this time, I attended countless Fast Draw meets and had the pleasure of observing at firsthand the reigning champion. At that time, he was not yet 20 years of age, and like my invention, Al Molina, Jr., a Latino from East Los Angeles. I was further privileged to meet his family, upon whom some of my characters are loosely based.

Finally, this book gave to a middle-aged Latino author the opportunity to relive some of those days when he too searched in vain for a hero among the ranks of all those suntanned, blue-eyed cowboys who galloped across the flickering screen of Saturday matinees at the Oasis Theater in Brooklyn, New York.

T.E.B.

Huntington Beach, California
1981

El Paso, 1916

The great gunfighter lay dying, his once firmly muscled body ravaged by the slow death that consumed him. No gunman's bullet, nor bandit's knife had been able to lay low Miguel Chacon, El Tigre. It had taken tuberculosis, the White Plague, to bring him down.

He shifted uncomfortably on the sweat-soaked linens of his rumpled cot bed. Immediately, the young cavalry trooper who sat at his bedside reached for a cloth. After dipping it in the tepid water of a large cracked bowl that stood atop the bedside table, he sponged El Tigre's brow. The dying gunfighter opened his eyes.

"Are you still here, Benito?" he asked in Spanish. "Will you not have trouble back at the fort for this?"

"I have permission, El Tigre," the young trooper answered. "My lieutenant understands."

"He is a good man for one so young," said El Tigre softly, "and brave to the point of foolishness. I admire him, in a way."

"Please, El Tigre. Don't talk. Save your strength," cautioned the young trooper.

"For what purpose?" said the gunfighter, smiling thinly. "To live another day, another hour in this wretched shack?" He gave a slight cough, which then gave way to spasms that wracked his body. The young trooper wiped the

blood from the lips of the dying man. Once the seizure had subsided, El Tigre whispered hoarsely to the young man.

"Benito, bring my pistol to me."

"What can you be thinking, El Tigre?" said the young trooper, shocked.

"No, no," the gunfighter said, a wisp of a smile brightening the deathly pallor of his face. "I do not wish to kill myself, hijito. *Do as I ask."*

The young trooper went to the far wall of the shack where a handsomely tooled belt and holster hung on a hook. He removed the Colt .45 Single-Action revolver from its resting place and brought the gun to the man in the bed.

"I have it here, El Tigre."

"Bueno," whispered the gunfighter "It is yours. I have no further use for it."

"But I cannot take this," said the young trooper. "Surely someone else . . ." He fell silent as the dying man raised his hand.

"There is no one else, Benito," he said. "I have neither wife nor son. You have been more family to me than I have ever known. I wish you to have my pistol. I have shown you how to use it. More important, I have shown you when not to use it . . . I would . . ."

Another fit of coughing seized El Tigre. This time, there was no stopping the spasms, nor could young Benito staunch the flow of the hemorrhage. In a few minutes' time, Miguel Chacon, the most feared and respected lawman the Mexican border states had ever known was dead.

The young trooper sat for hours at the bedside, silent tears running down his cheeks. Finally, as the sun began to set, he removed his hand from the cold clasp of the corpse that had been El Tigre. He covered the body with the still-damp sheet, then left to make arrangements for the funeral that he knew would be attended only by a few, those who remembered the days when El Tigre had been the salvation of this now-great city. For the year was 1916, and save for occasional raids by bandidos from across the border, peace had reigned for years. One rarely saw a man who was not a soldier wearing a sidearm in the streets, for the bandits were controlled by the United States Cavalry these days.

The young trooper snapped open his service holster and withdrew a pistol nearly identical to the one given him by El Tigre: a Colt .45 Single-Action. The barrel of El Tigre's pistol was longer by a few inches, and the front sight had been filed down. As he rode toward the city, he flung the newer Colt out into the sand and replaced it with El Tigre's Colt.

"I will never sell this gun, El Tigre," he said to the darkening hills. "I shall treasure it for the rest of my life."

One

Heart pounding, chest heaving, Teddy Machado ran. Past the Geneva Hotel for welfare tenants, past the Apollo 12 Bar and Grill, and still farther he ran. Clutched in the boy's hand was a brown paper bag containing only a quart of milk and six pork chops, the Machado family dinner for that evening.

Close behind him ran three members of The Barons, a street gang that virtually ruled the neighborhood where Teddy lived, on the Upper West Side of Manhattan. Teddy did not question the right of these hoodlums to terrorize and rob. He accepted it as a fact of life on West 81st Street.

The Barons weren't after the meager meal in Teddy's paper sack. Their goal was the cash he carried. Teddy had been cashing his father's unemployment check at García's Productos Tropicales, a grocery on Amsterdam Avenue. García deducted what groceries the Machado family had charged during the week, added the amount of Teddy's latest purchase and had handed the boy $75 change. García knew that he was breaking the law by cashing a pre-endorsed unemployment check. But it was by giving credit and rendering services of this sort that García was able to stay in business. The supermarkets offered lower prices, but García offered humanity.

As García counted out the last of Teddy Machado's change, the boy glanced toward the front window of the shop and a hard lump formed in the pit of his stomach. Staring through the window, and observing the entire transaction, was the brutal, porcine face of Rafael Guzman, the leader of the The Barons! Teddy watched in apprehension as Guzman waved to two of his underlings who lounged in a doorway across the avenue. Obediently, they crossed the street to join him in front of García's grocery. Teddy couldn't take his eyes from Guzman.

At 19 years of age, Rafael Guzman was physically a grown man. Six feet tall and more than 180 pounds, Guzman ruled The Barons and the neighborhood with a combination of street-acquired shrewdness and sheer physical terror. Some boys of Teddy's age whispered that Rafael had once killed a member of an opposing gang in a fight in nearby Central Park. Teddy believed it. And Guzman had just seen García count out $75 to Teddy!

Teddy knew that he was safe, so long as he remained inside García's store. A year ago, García had shot dead a would-be robber with the pistol he kept close to his cash drawer. Since then, even The Barons respected García. But Teddy also knew that he couldn't remain inside the store indefinitely. Sooner or later, he would have to try for a safe passage home.

García, too, had noticed the hoodlums gathered outside his shop window. "Do you want me to hold on to this money, Teddy?" he asked. "I can give it to your Mama and Papa next time I see them."

Teddy was tempted. But he thought of his father's many lectures to him about being a man, and not running from trouble. Lorenzo Machado had often said that running away was cowardly. And if Teddy left the money with García, one of his parents would have to come get it. That in turn, would prompt another lecture with slaps for punctuation.

"Thanks a lot, Mr. García," Teddy replied. "But I gotta go now."

García sighed heavily. He knew exactly what was going on. What can I do? he thought. I'm no cop. If I start getting one kid home safely, pretty soon it'll be the whole neighborhood. And sooner or later, I'll have to use the gun again.

The grocer thought back to the night a year past, the night of the robbery. His hands shook slightly as he recalled the terror of that night. He recalled the deafening explosion of the gun he had never before fired. His nausea when the robber sank to the floor, there to bleed out his life. The robber had been a boy not much older than 10-year-old Teddy Machado, but already addicted to heroin to the point where he would attempt robbery to satisfy his obscene need for the drug. But just now, García had an inspiration.

"Come over here, Teddy," said García, coming out from behind the counter and leading the boy to the rarely used side door of the store. "Look at this."

García pointed to a particularly uninteresting display of Tide detergent. He was aware that as he spoke, Guzman's eyes were still upon him. Curious as to what García was talking about, Teddy followed. To the boy's surprise, García suddenly kicked open the side door and roughly shoved Teddy outside into the street. "Run!" García exhorted. "Run like hell!"

Teddy required no further urging. His sneakers actually chirped against the pavement as he struck out running for home. García's ploy had gained Teddy no more than 25 feet between the boy and The Barons. But fear lent speed to Teddy's pumping legs and in seconds, he had put a hundred yards between himself and Rafael, his nearest pursuer.

Still farther Teddy ran. Now the entrance to the tenement where Teddy and his family lived was in sight. Teddy reached inside his T-shirt for the front door key, which hung about his neck on a length of stout butcher's twine. With only a second to spare, Teddy fumbled the key into the lock, opened the door, dashed inside and slammed the weighty bulk of the door in the face of Rafael Guzman. Teddy raced up the three flights of stairs, and in moments, had gained the safety of the Machado family apartment.

The boy stood inside the apartment, his back to the entry door, trying to catch his breath. As a stabbing pain in his side subsided, he slid slowly to the floor, his breath coming in great, panting sobs. Safe!

Teddy looked at the kitchen clock. It was half past four in the afternoon. His father would still be out, trying to find work. His mother was at work, waiting on tables at a nearby restaurant and wouldn't be home for an hour or more. The boy knew that his two younger sisters, Alicia and Iris, were at the Catholic Youth Center, playing in comparative safety. His mother would pick them up after work and see them home. As to Teddy's brother Rudi, almost 18, who knew what Rudi did after his part-time job was done? Rudi was becoming a man, Lorenzo Machado told Teddy, and was more independent of his family with each passing day.

Teddy was glad for the solitude of the empty apartment. For had Lorenzo Machado been at home, Teddy would have had to explain the circumstances that had brought him flushed, sweating and gasping for breath to the sanctuary of the Machado apartment. And of late, Lorenzo Machado had become extremely difficult to live with.

After 10 years of hard work for a garment manufacturer, driving a delivery truck, Machado had seen the firm go into bankruptcy, leaving Lorenzo only inadequate unemployment checks with which to support his family.

Each day, Lorenzo would read the early editions of the daily papers, searching for a job in the want ads. He would then subway downtown to where the employment agencies that hired temporary help were located. For the past five months, Lorenzo had spent his days in fruitless search. And when he returned each day empty-handed and pride-bruised to the Machado apartment, there was no living with Lorenzo's fits of depression and sudden outbursts of rage at inconsequential matters.

Teddy silently thanked Saint Jude that he was alone in the apartment this day. He put the pork chops and milk inside the venerable refrigerator in the kitchen, then snapped on the small black and white TV set in the living room. He seated himself in Lorenzo's chair in front of the set and waited as the TV whistled, whined and grudgingly produced a distorted image.

The familiar strains of the musical theme to *Gunsmoke* came scratchily through the tiny speaker of the old TV set. Teddy sat back and smiled. He liked *Gunsmoke*, and saw every rerun that the local station offered.

But Teddy's favorite version of *Gunsmoke* was shown on Channel 52, a UHF Spanish language station. For on this channel, Matt Dillon, Doc, Festus and Miss Kitty all spoke in Spanish! This especially pleased Teddy because on most English-speaking TV shows, anyone who spoke Spanish or with a Spanish accent was depicted as either a comic figure of ridicule or a cowardly villain.

Not that Teddy had given much thought to the way characters were portrayed on television shows. Far from it. He completely accepted this quirk of casting. Just as he accepted similar attitudes in the cartoon shows on which he was raised. There was Quick Draw McGraw's comical Mexican sidekick, Baba Looey, with his quaint accent, and other shows with characters just as harshly drawn. But Teddy didn't object; this was simply the way things were. The English-speaking episode of *Gunsmoke* was nearly over when Lorenzo Machado came through the door.

"Papa!" cried Teddy, getting up from Lorenzo's chair and accepting his father's hug and kiss. "You're early getting home!"

"And why not?" asked Lorenzo, grinning broadly. "I will need my sleep for work tonight!"

"A job? You found a job?" Teddy asked in delight.

"A job?" crowed Lorenzo. "Not just one. I have got myself two jobs, *hijito*!" Machado walked into the living room, turned off the television set and sat down in his favorite chair.

"Two jobs?" asked Teddy in wonderment. "But how can you work at two jobs, Papa?"

"It won't be easy, hijito," replied Lorenzo Machado. "Neither one of these jobs pays as much as my old job. I must work at both to make enough to keep the family going. And this will mean more responsibility for you, Teddy. You will have to get our dinner groceries each day and be the man of the house until I and your brother Rudi come home from work. Can you do this, Teddy?"

"I'll do my best, Papa," Teddy replied.

"*Bueno*," Lorenzo said. "I can ask no more than that of you. But *oye*, listen, Teddy. It will mean that I shall be gone from the house all the time, except when I am sleeping. There will be no more *Yanqui* games."

Teddy's face fell. Twice a month, during *beisbol* season, the boy and his father would take the long subway trip up to Yankee Stadium, in the Bronx, where Lorenzo would cheer rabidly for his beloved Yanquis. Teddy had always cherished those night games. Once, Lorenzo had caught a foul ball, hit high into the second tier of inexpensive seats where they habitually sat. Teddy kept the ball in his bureau drawer, in the room he shared with his brother Rudi. Teddy would miss these excursions to the Bronx sorely. But the boy smiled and said: "I understand, Papa. It's okay."

"That's my boy," Lorenzo replied. "And as soon as I get a decent job instead of these two bad ones, we'll be going to the Yanqui games again. This I promise."

But as months went by, circumstances eroded Lorenzo's fine intentions. He lost one of his jobs, then found another low-paying one to take its place. Only to lose his day job. A profound sense of futility and disgust began to permeate Lorenzo's being. His periodic depressions and irrational rages began anew. He was as a trapped animal. He needed two jobs to stay alive. But when he held two jobs, he was unable to find time to seek other, better work.

It seemed that holidays and family occasions were the worst times. Each successive child's birthday when Lorenzo couldn't afford so much as a small gift for a son or daughter would end with harsh words or a bitter argument between Lorenzo and his wife, Luisa.

Teddy strove bravely to keep his promise to his father. But in the same way Lorenzo was a prisoner of financial circumstances, so was Teddy a prisoner in the Machado apartment. For outside the family's flat, on the street, lurked daily terror in the shape of The Barons. Each day, Teddy would take a circuitous route to school with the aim of avoiding any contact with the street gang. But their favorite hangout place seemed to be the schoolyard of the very grammar school Teddy attended.

The boy was monumentally relieved when school ended for the summer. And Teddy often wondered what he would have done if Luisa Machado had not enrolled Alicia and Iris at Saint Gregory's parochial school. She brought the girls there each day on her way to work, and picked them up on her way home. If Teddy had to escort his sisters to the same school he attended, he wouldn't have been able to run from The Barons. Alicia and Iris were too small to be as fleet of foot as Teddy. Once school ended, Teddy gained a temporary respite from harassment by The Barons, save when he made his trips to García's Productos Tropicales. Even then, he would often wait for hours before entering García's store, making sure that none of The Barons was near.

Then Lorenzo fell ill. The steady grind of two full-time jobs with minimal sleep had taken its toll of the man's health. By sheer willpower, Lorenzo hung onto his day job, but once more, the night job with its essential income was lost. Daily, Lorenzo helplessly watched himself sink deeper and deeper into debt.

"I can get a job, Papa," Teddy said to Lorenzo one evening. "I could maybe deliver groceries for Señor García. Or maybe shine shoes."

"No, Teddy," Lorenzo had replied. "You are only 10 years old. You cannot get working papers. García would get in trouble with the law if he took you on. And *además*, no son of mine shines shoes. I had to do it when I was a boy. It is demeaning. It takes away a man's pride, his *amor própio*. No, my son. I will find something, some way to earn more money."

But again, Lorenzo's hopes fell short of reality. And once more the bitter arguments between Lorenzo and Luisa Machado were renewed. One night, as Teddy lay in bed alongside his brother Rudi, who was able to sleep regardless of any disruptions, Teddy was awakened by loud, harsh words coming from the kitchen.

Teddy slipped out of bed and walked soundlessly down the long hall of the family's railroad flat. He crept past the room his two sisters shared and the empty bedroom of his parents. He stood just out of sight of his parents as they sat at the kitchen table arguing.

"Are you saying that I cannot support my family?" Lorenzo shouted. "We have to take in strangers, boarders?"

"No, *querido*," Luisa Machado said softly. "Not a boarder. He is your own *abuelo*, your grandfather. That's hardly a stranger."

"Benito Machado has been a stranger to my family ever since he abandoned my grandmother. When my father and uncle were just kids," Lorenzo replied heatedly. "Now he wants to come and stay with us."

"That's not what his letter says, Lorenzo," Luisa said. "I suppose that it is of my doing, though. You see, he volunteered to come here after I wrote to him asking for a small loan, until you could find a good job—"

"You *what*?" roared Lorenzo Machado. "You dared ask my grandfather for money? Since I was a boy, my father, God rest his soul, drummed one thing into my head: Benito Machado had no use for his family when he ran out on us. And we have no use for Benito Machado! I wouldn't ask that man for the sweat off his . . . nose!"

"You never spoke so strongly about this before, querido," said Luisa. "Otherwise I would not have done it. But nevertheless, it is done. And now what will I do with this check for three hundred dollars that he has sent to us?"

"Tear it up!" snapped Lorenzo. "I take no charity from Benito Machado!"

"But it isn't charity, 'Renzo," Luisa Machado said. "It's his first month's rent in advance. He is on his way to *Nueva York* from California, even as we speak. And querido, we need this money badly. Our rent is a month late. If we don't pay soon, we will be out on the street. Then you will take charity. You will have to!"

"What will I do with this woman?" Lorenzo asked of the ceiling in an anguished tone. He drained his can of *Cerveza Schaefer*, the one daily luxury he allowed himself.

"Very well, woman," he said. "I will accept this check. But only because I have no choice."

"I knew you would see reason, querido," Luisa Machado said, getting up and putting her arms around Machado as he sat at the table. She kissed him lightly on the neck and nipped gently at his ear. Lorenzo halfheartedly moved away.

"I do not see reason. I see only necessity," Lorenzo said. "And if there is one bit of trouble with the old man . . . ."

"There will be no trouble," said Luisa, renewing her nuzzling of Lorenzo's neck. "He says in his letter that all he wants is to spend time with what remains of his family. Surely you wouldn't deny an old, old man this simple pleasure?"

"But where will we put him, *muñeca?*" Lorenzo asked. "Where will the old man sleep?"

"He can take the girls' room, 'Renzo. They are still young. They can share the convertible sofa in the living room. Oh, it will all work out. You'll see."

"*Sí,*" Lorenzo agreed darkly. "*Vamos a ver.*" As he stood up, Teddy heard the chair scrape against the linoleum floor of the kitchen and knew that his parents were about to retire for the night. Teddy quickly made his way back to his bed, where undisturbed by all the noise, Rudi slept on. For a long time, Teddy lay in the darkness, thinking.

My father's grandfather, Teddy thought. His abuelo. That makes him my . . . Teddy searched for the word in Spanish. Like most New York-born Puerto Ricans, Teddy's primary language was English. What Spanish he spoke was comprised of 50-odd phrases, liberally larded with Americanisms. Educators call it *Spanglish*; an uneasy blend of English and Spanish that is proper usage in neither language.

Finally, the word came to Teddy. "That makes him my *bisabuelo,*" he said aloud, not realizing he had spoken. Rudi grunted and rolled over in his sleep. In a short time, Teddy too had fallen asleep.

TWO

Teddy answered the door that day, the afternoon after his parents had quarreled. He looked up and saw an honest-to-God cowboy standing in the tenement hallway. A shade taller than six feet, and despite his years, erect as a ramrod, the old man was dressed in an expensively cut western-style suit. He wore elaborately tooled cowboy boots. On his head was a pearl gray Stetson hat that had a high, rounded, unblocked crown. The brim wasn't folded over, like a movie cowboy's, either. It was flat as a dinner plate, all around the domed crown.

"Howdy, *muchacho*," said the apparition in the doorway. "You must be Teodoro. I'm your bisabuelo, Benito Machado. Shake, pardner!"

That day began the happiest years in Teddy's young life. For what had begun as a temporary arrangement for the Machado family's troubled finances, blossomed into a three-year stay. Space was arranged according to Luisa's plan to accommodate Benito Machado.

It was fortunate for the family that although the tenement apartment was small, it did boast three bedrooms. A rare stroke of luck had brought the Machados to Manhattan from the Bronx. A distant cousin was moving back to Puerto Rico. The Machados, having the same family name, moved in and retained the old, city controlled rental rates. Had the landlord known he was housing a different group of Machados, the rent would have been raised fourfold.

The old man moved into the third bedroom and soon had it decorated to his own taste. Teddy loved visiting in the old man's room. Benito Machado had hung a large picture of General John

Pershing on one wall. Benito had served under Pershing in Texas during the time of the Mexican Border Wars.

Facing the picture of General Pershing was a large color poster of the actor George C. Scott in his film role as General George S. Patton. Benito would have preferred a picture of the real General Patton, but as he explained to Teddy, it was easier to get a picture of George Scott. Teddy's bisabuelo had actually known the real General Patton in Mexico. Back then, Benito told Teddy, he wasn't a general yet; just a lieutenant.

Benito Machado had served in two world wars and had retired on his pension thirty years before, after the close of World War II. His pension wasn't grand, but by the standards of either San Juan, Puerto Rico, or *barrio Nueva York*, he was well off. His needs were Spartan, a hangover from his military days, and since retiring he had also worked to augment his pension. By the time his Social Security pension began paying out, Benito Machado was set for life.

But to Teddy, Benito Machado's room was luxuriously appointed. In addition to the two generals' portraits, on the opposite wall hung a U.S. Cavalry saber. Below that was the proof that Teddy's bisabuelo had indeed been a real cowboy. It was a well worn, single-holster gunbelt. And hanging in the holster, just like in the movies, was a long-barreled Colt .45 revolver! There were even real cartridges in the little leather holders on the sides of the gunbelt.

The change in the Machado household wasn't simply physical, either. At last Teddy had someone with whom to share his passion for all things western, for Benito Machado loved westerns as much as Teddy did.

But being a product of the true Wild West, Benito was openly scornful of most TV westerns. He thought that the reruns of *The Rifleman* were so bad as to be laughable.

"*¡Mira!*" he would cry, tugging at Teddy's sleeve. "Look at this Lucas McCaine fool! He must crank that silly rifle of his each time before he fires. A real *pistolero* would shoot him full of holes. He would never get to fire a second round. *¡Que chanza!* What a joke!"

"What would a real sheriff do, bisabuelo?" Teddy asked.

"That would depend," the old man said reflectively. "If he was wise, he would wait until the bandido was asleep, in a hotel or a rooming house. Our sheriff would first station two armed men in the hall, outside the bandido's room. . . ."

"Then what, bisabuelo?"

"Then our lawman would sneak into the sleeping bandido's room, through the window. He would then knock the man over the head with an ax handle and cart him off to jail."

"With no shooting?"

"Only if the bad man woke and went for his pistol."

"But is that fair, bisabuelo? Getting a man when he's asleep?"

"What is fair, hijito?" said Benito Machado with a smile and a philosophical shrug. "To wake up this bad man and ask him to draw? *Tontería*: foolishness. There is always going to be someone who can draw and fire a pistol faster than you."

The old man evidently enjoyed Teddy's look of dismay at such nonsporting behavior, for he added: "What's more, if this man of which we speak was truly fast with a pistol, I would take no chance at all. I would shoot him through the window. With a shotgun. It is a marvelous weapon for such things. It can see in the dark."

"I don't understand," Teddy said. "How can a shotgun see at all?"

"It's only an expression, *chico*. Of course a gun cannot see. But a shotgun fires many slugs at the same time; a pistol only one. You do not have to aim a shotgun precisely. The slugs from a shotgun scatter over a wide area. You will hit anything in front of the muzzle when you squeeze the triggers. Yes, for a darkened room a shotgun is best." He looked with wry amusement at Teddy's expression and went on watching the television set.

Teddy and old Benito became inseparable. On Saturdays, they would go to any movie house that advertised a western film. The authentic western films delighted Benito. He would point out to Teddy actual places he himself had seen while in the U.S. Cavalry. And when the films were not authentic, the old man would jeer and hoot with scorn at the errors.

"Look at that!" he would cry, grabbing at Teddy's shoulder in the darkness. "That Indian pony . . . that horse has iron shoes. Real Indians didn't shoe their horses. And these so-called Sioux Indians . . . they are wearing Dakota warpaint."

Or: "That cavalry trooper is wearing a Navy pistol." Then smiling, he would add: "It's just as well. He rides like a sailor!"

One Saturday afternoon, after seeing a double feature of *High Noon* and *Gunfight at the O.K. Corral*, Benito and Teddy decided to walk from the Edison Theater on 97th Street to the

Machado apartment on 81st. As they strolled down Amsterdam Avenue, the old man began to hum "Home On the Range."

"I know that song, bisabuelo," Teddy said happily, and began to sing: "Home, home on the range/Where the deer and the cantaloupe play. . . ."

"What was that you sang, hijito?" asked Benito Machado. The boy repeated what he had sung. When he came to the chorus, Benito held up a hand and said gently to Teddy, "No, no hijito. It is *antelope*, not *cantaloupe*."

"Well, I know what a cantaloupe is, bisabuelo. But what is an antelope?"

The old man sighed and took Teddy's face between his large, weathered hands. "*¡Que lastima!* What a shame that you do not know what an antelope is! I must buy some books for you, Teddy."

Benito introduced Teddy to the great western writers: Zane Grey, Luke Short, and the flamboyant Max Brand. He also referred Teddy to the more authentic Harry Drago and Louis L'Amour. When Lorenzo Machado began to object to his son constantly reading western novels, Luisa was quick to point out that Teddy's grades in Reading had improved immensely.

And for three glorious seasons, Benito took Teddy to the rodeo at Madison Square Garden. It was at the rodeo that Benito bought for his great-grandson a matched set of pearl-handled cap pistols. They were shiny-plated, and the cylinder would swing out, so one could load them with dummy bullets that contained small black powder caps. These wonders of the toymaker's art were direct replicas of the Colt .45 that hung on Benito's bedroom wall. But the old man would not allow Teddy to strap on the gunbelt that came with the toy guns. He sneered at the imitation silver chasings and the cheap leather.

He took Teddy to a small store not far from Madison Square Garden. There, for the first time, Teddy saw a genuine leatherwork shop. What wonders filled that store! Gunbelts, holsters, fancy buckles. And the gorgeously worked Mexican silver saddles! In still another section of the store were boots and hats. Real 10-gallon cowboy hats, not the imitations sold at the concession stands at the rodeo. And above all, there was the scent of the Old West in the air: leather, saddle soap and glue.

Benito Machado bought Teddy a black leather and silver chased gunbelt with two holsters. He also bought his great-grandson a pair of matching black and silver boots. Teddy was beside himself with joy when the old man led him to the part of the store where the hats were displayed.

Teddy's hat was to be a Stetson, the old man was firm on that. And although Teddy's new boots were black, Benito Machado insisted that the boy's hat be light gray in color. When Teddy asked why, the old man explained how important a good hat is to a cowboy.

"A lot of the time, hijito, your hat is the only roof you have. It should reflect the heat of the noon sun. That's why a black hat isn't good. Your hat must also keep the sun out of your eyes and off the back of your neck so you don't get sunburned there."

Teddy was also surprised to learn that a real cowboy's hat doesn't have a curly brim, or a shape to its crown when new. It comes out of the box with a high, unshaped crown and the brim flat as a dinner plate.

"The shape you desire in your hat is what you choose to make it," explained Benito. "When you get your new hat, you shape and tie the brim, then dent the crown the way you want it. After that, you wet it and let the hat dry in the hot sun. When it dries, you have the shape that your hat will keep. Your hat is your *marca personal*, your trademark. I have seen thousands of cowboys in my life, but rarely the same shape to each one's hat."

"But bisabuelo, you wear your hat like it just came out of the box."

"True," said the old man. "With so many choices to make, I made the simplest. The way I wear my sombrero is the best for me. On the hottest days, the straight brim keeps the sun off my face and neck. In the rain, the water doesn't trickle down my neck.

"The crown I wear so high because it puts space between the top of my head and the top of my hat. That way, I don't fry my brains in the hot sun, like these movie cowboys would. The hats they wear, they would fry, Teddy. They would sizzle like bacon!" Teddy decided that he would wear his sombrero exactly as his great-grandfather did.

Once Benito was assured that Teddy's hat was the proper size, he wouldn't allow the boy to wear it. Nor would he disclose to Teddy the contents of the mysterious packages he had acquired while Teddy had gazed, rapt, at the showcases in the store. And instead of taking the IRT subway home, Benito hailed a taxicab. The two rode home in style, with the unidentified packages tantalizingly close to Teddy in the backseat of the cab.

When they arrived, no one was home; not even Teddy's sisters. A note from Luisa on the kitchen table said that the family would return shortly. They were visiting friends on West 92nd Street. Benito and Teddy went to the old man's room.

Once inside, the old man spread out his purchases across the bed and swung open his closet door, which had an old full-length mirror hanging on it. He began opening the packages, one at a time, and with each new disclosure, Teddy's eyes grew wider.

There was a black western shirt, matching vest and whip-cord trousers. Teddy scrambled into the new clothes as fast as he could shed his jeans, sneakers and T-shirt. He had a bit of trouble pulling on his new black and silver boots; the leather was stiff. When finally the real leather gunbelt was strapped to his waist and his cap pistols holstered, Benito led Teddy to the full-length mirror. Then, as an archbishop would place a crown on the head of an annointed monarch, Benito gently lowered the boy's new Stetson atop Teddy's head.

Remembering that cowboys don't cry, no matter what, Teddy fought back his tears of joy. Shiny-eyed, he regarded his reflection in the old, flaked mirror. Then, suddenly, he made his move, drawing both pistols at his image in the glass.

"Bam bam!" cried Teddy.

"*¡Bien hecho!*" laughed Benito Machado. "Well done, Teddy!"

"Bam, bam!" Teddy repeated.

"El Tigre. . . ." Benito Machado said to himself, more than to Teddy.

"Pardon, bisabuelo?" the boy asked.

"I was thinking that you remind me of someone," smiled the old man. "A lawman I knew in Texas many years ago. His name was Miguel Chacon, but everyone called him El Tigre: The Tiger."

"How do I remind you of him, bisabuelo?"

"For one thing, he dressed as you are dressed now: all in black, with a gray hat. All the Mexicans thought he was a Mexican as well. But he wasn't. He was Cuban. None of that mattered, though. For Mexican, Cuban or whatever, no one fooled with El Tigre. Not if he wanted to live, that is."

The old man pointed to the holster and pistol hanging on the wall, and said to Teddy: "I often think of El Tigre. That is his Peacemaker Colt you see there. He gave it to me the day he died."

"Who shot him, bisabuelo?"

"No one. He died of tuberculosis. There was no gunfighter who could have killed El Tigre face to face. Sometimes, I think his spirit lives on, in that old pistol."

The old man shook his head as though to clear it of unwanted memories.

"But just now," he said briskly, "I am thirsty. Let me go see if my grandson has left me any beer in the refrigerator."

After Benito Machado left the bedroom, Teddy stayed behind, admiring the handsome figure he cut as a cowboy. He examined his front view and both profiles. He nearly dislocated his neck trying to see what he looked like from behind. Then suddenly he whirled, drawing both cap pistols from the holsters at his sides.

"You just had a close call, pardner," he advised his reflection. "Don't try it again."

Three

Luisa Machado thought Teddy looked marvelous in his western garb. Lorenzo was scandalized.

"*Madre de Diós*, Luisa," he said to his wife after Teddy had gone to bed, and the old man was watching the *Late News* in the living room. "Do you realize how much money the old man spent on the crap Teddy is wearing?"

"It's the abuelo's money to spend, querido," reminded Luisa.

"All the same, I could have got the boy a winter coat, two pairs of Thom McAn's, and had money left over."

"Teddy has a good winter coat. And his sneakers. And leather shoes for church on Sunday."

"Then, if the old *loco* wants to spend money so much, let him put some food on the table," replied Lorenzo Machado.

"He already pays his share and more," Luisa said. "You know, 'Renzo, I think you are hurt in your pride. That your grandfather could spend money on such things for your son, when you can't afford to."

Lorenzo Machado pushed his chair back from the table angrily. It fell to the kitchen floor with a slam. "Nonsense!" he snapped. "I just work too hard for my money to see good dollars poured down a rathole!"

"Your son is hardly a rathole," said Benito Machado from the doorway. Attracted by the arguing, he had come silently to the kitchen and overheard.

"Further," Benito Machado said, "I will forgive you for calling me crazy, for it's obvious that you understand neither your son nor me."

"I understand what it is to work for a living. It is a serious business, abuelo. And when one works as hard as I do . . . to see money thrown away. It angers me."

"As well it should. But I have thrown nothing away. Any young man should own a good Stetson hat, a belt and a fine pair of boots. The cap pistols, I admit were frivolous."

"But dammit, abuelo," cried Lorenzo Machado. "This isn't Waco, Arizona. This is Nueva York, and we don't have any cowboys here!"

"*Claro*; obviously," smiled the old man. "Perhaps it would be a better place to live if we did."

"I'm not joking," said Lorenzo to his grandfather. "And if you find life in Nueva York with us so terrible . . ."

"There are other places?" asked the old man, raising his eyebrows.

"*¡Precísamente!*" replied Lorenzo Machado.

Benito Machado smiled sadly and sat down at the kitchen table. He turned to Luisa and said: "Muñeca, in my room, in the top drawer of the bureau, is a big, old book. Under it, is a flat black box. And on the top shelf of the closet is a bottle of Ron Rico 151-proof rum. Would you please go and get these things for me?"

The two men sat in silence, while Luisa went to the old man's room. Lorenzo shifted uncomfortably under the steady dark-eyed gaze of his grandfather. Luisa soon returned, and over two jelly tumblers of the fiery, overproof rum, the men began to talk. Luisa, who was strict church, drank a coke.

"Lorenzo," began Benito Machado, "I came here three years ago to spend my final years with family. The idea came to me late in life, and I can see that like many of the ideas that have moved me across this earth, it was *una quimera*; a dream." He took a sip of rum. "Perhaps I felt guilty about abandoning your grand-mother and your father. Though over the years, I always sent money to her in Puerto Rico. It was money I sent that allowed your father to come to Nueva York. I had great hopes for your father—"

"My father was a good man, and a hard worker," said Lorenzo, defensively.

"Claro, claro," soothed the old man. "No one disputes that. But I had hoped that he would be something more. That he would have a sense of adventure, as I did."

Benito Machado opened the large scrapbook that lay upon the table. The first page revealed snapshots of a very young man in Army uniform. Benito Machado gazed at the yellowing photographs, smiled and shook his head.

"I sometimes wonder what became of that wild young *hombre* I was," Benito said softly. "I know that even today, he lives inside me. As rash and young as ever. But alas, the body he inhabits won't serve his youth as it once did." The old man poured himself a drink.

"When I left Puerto Rico, so many years ago," he continued, "not many men went to the mainland. That was not their dream. Young men my age thought of one day owning a *finca*, a little farm. And as they spent their years cutting cane on a landlord's land, they dreamed of the farms they would never own. I recognized this fact early on: A working man will never be a rich man. One who works for wages will always work for wages."

"I have heard that said," nodded Lorenzo in agreement.

"Then you have heard the truth," concluded Benito Machado. "Or at least the truth as I saw it so long ago. I saw a chance to escape that circle of work, wages and death, and I grabbed it! In 1907, I was 17 years of age and already the father of two sons. As Puerto Rico was newly made American territory, and I a newly made American citizen, I enlisted in the U.S. Army.

"I thought that I would be stationed at a Puerto Rican garrison. I had seen the *gringo* soldiers. With their fine clothes, good food and leather boots; not a poor man's sandals. Compared with what I was able to provide as a farmhand, I assumed that we could live well, your *abuela*, your father and Uncle Ramon. I already spoke English of the sort soldiers spoke," Benito smiled widely. "And there were, of course, the poor sainted nuns who tried to teach me in school. *¡Ay!* I was a wild one, I'm afraid."

"So you simply left your family?" asked Lorenzo.

"I had no trouble being accepted by the Army," continued the old man, ignoring Lorenzo's remark. "But I had trouble being accepted by the soldiers as a man. To the regular Army men, I was dirt. Oh, yes, I could clean stables and shovel shit. I could work in a kitchen and haul garbage. But a soldier, I was not.

"It was: 'Here, Spicky, do this!' or 'Hey, Spick, do that!' When a chance came for Spanish-speaking troops to fight bandidos in Mexico, I applied and got the post. I thank God for that day. For, when I got out West, I wasn't a Spick. I was a real man, with *dos huevos*."

Benito Machado tenderly picked up the long flat box that lay on the table. He placed it gently across the pages of his scrapbook and slowly opened it. Inside, there was an Army decoration.

"Mira, Lorenzo," the old man said. "This is a Bronze Star. It is a decoration given to heros in combat. You will see it is engraved with my name and then-rank of corporal. It doesn't say Spick anywhere, does it? Out West, it is what you do, not what you come from that makes you a man."

"And you wish to make a cowboy of my son," said Lorenzo, "because you were successful out West, years ago? Abuelo, the world has changed since those days. Today, one works and saves. Maybe someday, one could buy a small house, perhaps a little business—"

"Crap!" roared the old man, slamming his palm against the tabletop.

"Listen to yourself; what you are saying! You will hear the same fools in the Puerto Rican canefields talking. What's the difference between you and some shoeless *campesino* in Puerto Rico, so many years ago?"

"And I hear a silly old man, talking about a world that died over fifty years ago!" retorted Lorenzo, heatedly. "And moreover," he added, "I will have no more of this nonsense drummed into my son's head. Remember, old man, he is *my* son, not yours!"

"He would be better off, were he mine," snapped Benito Machado.

"That may, or may not be," replied Lorenzo. "But while you and he are both under my roof, my wishes will be respected. Do you hear me, abuelo?"

"All too well, *muchacho*," said Benito Machado, finishing his rum and standing. "I will be gone from here by the time you get home tomorrow night."

"Fine with me!" shouted Lorenzo.

And despite protests from Luisa and the children, the old man, true to his word, left the Machado household the next day. But not before he said a special goodbye to Teddy. The boy had put on his new western outfit, complete to the cap pistols in the gunbelt. And forgetting the interdiction against tears, Teddy wept openly. If the old man hadn't swallowed hard, the boy would have seen Benito's tears, as well.

"You are fine looking, and you are a good boy, Teddy," Benito Machado said. "And one day, you will be a fine man." He put his large, liver-spotted hands on each of the boy's shoulders.

"But remember this, Teodoro. Your father is a good man, too. He is just not the same sort of man as we are. If he were an animal, Lorenzo would be a good, steady workhorse.

"You and I; we are different. We are like fine Arabian horses, fit for a general to ride. And like such beautiful animals, we have inside us a streak of wildness. It is a spark; a precious spirit of adventure that lives inside us, hijito.

"Don't let the bastards rob you of your spark! If you have a dream, pursue it. It may be a rainbow, but dammit, boy, chase it! Live your life with your whole heart and soul. And never, never give up your dreams. For it is our dreams that separate men from the animals of the field. Always be a fleet Arabian, and never pull a plow!"

Benito Machado took a white handkerchief from his back pocket and blew his nose with a resounding honk. "I must go now, Teddy," he said gently. "No, don't see me to the door. Stay here. I don't say goodbye well."

He turned abruptly, picked up his two bulky suitcases as though they were filled with feathers, and strode erectly from the room.

Teddy remained in the now bare-walled hall bedroom. He heard the front door of the apartment close. He walked over to the wall where his great-grandfather's saber and pistol had hung. He touched the spot where the picture of General Pershing had hung. He wept, quietly, but in great gasping heaves that shook his narrow frame. Then, as steel is tempered by water, so a hardening process began inside Teddy Machado. He took his face from his cupped hands and stood erect. He faced his reflection in the mirror. The two sixguns at his side, the Stetson on his head.

In that moment, a new Teddy Machado was born. His eyes narrowed into dark, steely slits, his hands hung like hovering birds above the handles of his twin .45's. He became, on the day Benito Machado left, a man whose name would ever strike terror in the hearts of badmen and bandidos: El Tigre!

Four

As Teddy ("El Tigre") Machado rounded the corner of West 81st Street and Amsterdam Avenue, he hitched up his gunbelt and set his 10-gallon hat firmly upon his head. His dark eyes narrowed as he noted the approach of the morning stagecoach to Boston. No, he was safe. Sometimes a bushwhacker would try to pick him off from a window of the passing stage. But today, all the windows were closed. The stage passed by with a roar and spewed a noxious nimbus of diesel exhaust into the air.

El Tigre continued his walk down Amsterdam Avenue. Not much of a breeze today. That was good. A breeze could raise a cloud of dust and spoil your aim.

"*Buenos días*, sheriff!" called Mr. García from the doorway of García's Productos Tropicales. The hard-eyed sheriff nodded in return greeting.

"Crazy dam' kid," said García to himself as he went back into his corner grocery store.

El Tigre resumed his morning rounds. As ever, he was careful to stroll only the middle of the sidewalk. Ambushers and owlhoots often hid in the doorways. But the solid feel of the two pearl-handled .45's at his sides was reassuring. After all, he was the most-feared peace officer on the danger-filled West Side of Manhattan. Gunslingers and bandidos knew it was El Tigre's turf, and mostly they stayed clear.

A sudden movement from a doorway! El Tigre pivoted, and with a motion that spoke hours of practice, his Colt was half clear of leather. Then, he saw it was only Mr. Casparian, off to work at the Red Apple Supermarket where he was daytime cashier.

"Morning, Marshal Dillon," said Mr. Casparian. He always made that same mistake. Dillon hadn't been marshal for years now. Ever since El Tigre had come to town.

Even Matt Dillon had to admit that there was no one faster or more fearless on the West Side. The big marshal had seen El Tigre in action only once. But once had been enough. He'd handed his star over to El Tigre, saying:

"I been waitin' all these years to retire, El Tigre. But I was never sure Dodge City would be safe, once I left. Well, she's all yours, now. Me and Miss Kitty is gettin' married. We'll be retirin' to Florida, just as soon as the stage to Kennedy Airport gits here."

El Tigre had seen them both off on the stage. It was too bad that Doc and Festus had moved away to Astoria, in Queens. They would have wanted to be there. But that had been long ago, when El Tigre was only 13 years old. Now, two years later, Mr. Casparian still called El Tigre by the old marshal's name. Not that it mattered. So long as the bad guys knew whose town it was.

El Tigre walked faster now. It was already 8:15. He was due at the Brandeiss School in 15 minutes, and he still hadn't checked First National City Bank on Broadway. El Tigre shook his head. The guard, Di Giorgio, was old. El Tigre was sure that the old man hadn't fired his pistol in years. One day, he thought, a raiding party would knock over that bank just as easy as the free lunch counter at the Long Branch Saloon. Umm. Ought to check out the Long Branch, he thought. They'll be opening about now.

He grunted in dissatisfaction at the sign over the Long Branch, which still read Rosa Azul Bar & Grill. When the marshal and Miss Kitty had left Dodge, Ismael Rivera had bought the Long Branch. Rivera had listened respectfully when El Tigre had told him that the Rosa Azul would always be the Long Branch. Rivera had even promised that he'd get a new sign. But for one reason or another, the new sign had never gone up.

El Tigre peered into the Long Branch window at street level. Rivera was already inside, setting up the bar for a new day. The light was lit over the pool table, and a couple of tinhorns were having a game of eight ball. El Tigre snorted in disgust at the loafers. Then again, he thought, they're citizens, too. They get my protection whether they respect the law or not.

Rivera glanced up from his work at the bar. He saw El Tigre through the street window and waved cheerily in greeting. Then Rivera spoke to the tinhorns at the pool table. El Tigre couldn't hear what was said, but the two loafers left their game and smiled at El Tigre as he passed the window. They all smiled widely.

"Okay, you bad guys," Ismael Rivera said to the pool shooters. "The day is now official. The sheriff just passed by."

The pool shooter nearest Rivera roared with laughter. "What

the hell was *that*?" he asked between gasps.

"That's Lorenzo Machado's kid," Rivera explained. "I think he's about 15 now, and still playing cowboys and Indians." Rivera made the universal gesture of a finger rotating next to his temple. "He's a little loco, that one. But he don't harm nobody. Those are just cap guns he wears."

"Diós mío," said the pool shooter, "if I had a kid like that, I'd worry. I know Lorenzo Machado. He's a serious man. He always works . . . . How'd he end up with a son who's crazy?"

"How does anyone go crazy in Nueva York?" shrugged Rivera.

"Just living here and trying to hold a job?" offered the other pool shooter.

"How would you know?" came back Rivera. The three men laughed again.

But by now, the sheriff was too far away to hear the laughter. He entered the schoolyard at Brandeiss School just as the 8:30 bell rang. The Barons were in the yard. He could see several members of the street gang he had reason to know by sight: Paco, Rafael, Geek and Ramon. Adelita Ramirez was hanging onto Rafael, the leader of The Barons. To El Tigre's practiced eye, that meant the rest of the gang couldn't be far away. A slight movement near the Student's Entrance caught his eye.

Sure enough, The Barons were waiting to bushwhack him. But El Tigre, though he had the courage of a thousand men, was no fool, either. When The Barons had first got out of hand, ambushing the sheriff for his lunch money, and humiliation of humiliations, had even taken his sixguns for a time, El Tigre had sent telegrams to Wyatt Earp, Bat Masterson and Doc Holliday. It was simply a matter of time before those three famous lawmen rode into Dodge.

Once his deputies arrived, El Tigre promised himself grimly, The Barons would curse the day they ambushed him. With Wyatt, Bat and Doc at his side, El Tigre would clean out The Barons, once and for all.

But assessing the situation, El Tigre decided that now wasn't the time for a confrontation between him and The Barons. He felt the dry rustle of the two one-dollar bills in his pocket. The lunch money his mother had given to him. It had to be lunch money, he explained to his mother. For, with a brown paper lunch bag in his hand, he could only use one of his pearl-handled .45's at a time. It made him a walking target, that lunch bag.

And having been ambushed by The Barons once before, he

was aware the gang knew he daily carried the precious gold shipment for lunch. It could mean *mucho* trouble. El Tigre sighed deeply. Then his face brightened. He remembered that the Selwyn Theater on 42nd Street was showing a double feature of *Shane* and *The Last Gunfighter*. If El Tigre got to the theater before the prices changed at noon, he'd have enough coins left to buy a candy bar for lunch. With a grunt of determination, the lawman turned on his heel and made for the train station. A thin smile of anticipation played about his lips as he walked. Ahead lay the railroad station, clearly marked: IRT Subway Downtown . . . .

The slap caught Teddy Machado full in the face as he entered the apartment door. His left ear rang from the impact of his father's hand.

"Where the hell were you today?" shouted Lorenzo Machado. "The high school called again!" He grabbed Teddy and spun him into the center of the tiny tenement apartment living room. "And turn that dam' TV off!" he cried to his wife, who was ironing and watching *Family Feud*.

Luisa Machado rushed between her son and husband, the TV set still blaring. "For God's sake, Lorenzo!" she cried. "Let the boy answer before you hit him. I'm sure there's a reason . . . ."

"He's not a boy!" said Lorenzo Machado angrily. "He's almost a grown man. When I was 16, I was working and bringing money into the house. When I was 19, married. Now, I work my tail off so he can go to school and amount to something. And what thanks do I get? This big *bobo* doesn't go to the school. All he wants to do is play cowboys!" He turned and glared at Teddy, who was picking up his Stetson hat from the floor where it had fallen.

* * * * * *

As El Tigre brushed the dust from his fallen Stetson, he realized he was in deep trouble. But he couldn't show a trace of fear. Even though Ike Clanton was knocking him around. The Clantons were a family of notorious outlaws who terrorized the West. And among the three brothers, Ike, the eldest, was considered the toughest. For now, El Tigre had to take the abuse. But once Doc, Wyatt and Bat got his telegram, things would change . . . pronto.

* * * * * *

"Answer me, dammit!" said Lorenzo Machado to his son. "Where were you today, instead of school?"

"Around," answered El Tigre, his steely eyes speaking defiance, as he brushed a speck of lint from his 10-gallon hat.

"That does it!" raged Lorenzo Machado. He knocked the boy's hat from his hand and kicked it across the room. "This is the end of my patience! If you won't go to school, you go to work. I'm going to see about working papers for you. If you can finish this session of school, it's the last! You'll get a job. Maybe then you'll understand what the real world is about!"

"No, Lorenzo, no!" protested Luisa Machado. "He's a good boy. He's just a dreamer, is all . . . ."

"Then let him dream on his own money," snapped Lorenzo. "No way I work six days a week to support an idiot son. Look at the size of him. Almost as tall as me, and he's still playing make-believe!"

Luisa didn't comment on the point of Teddy's size. At 15½ years of age, the boy was five feet ten inches tall, though painfully thin. Lorenzo Machado hardly appeared to be related to his son. The elder Machado was only an inch taller, though nearly a hundred pounds heavier. Where Lorenzo's face was broad and his nose betrayed evidence of childhood griefs and battles, spreading generously across his face, Teddy had fine, almost delicate features. Lorenzo's hair was shiny black and straight; Teddy's tightly curled into a semi-Afro, comically distorted in shape by the Stetson hat he wore everywhere but to bed. Machado regarded his son with contempt, then turned to his wife.

"Do you know he's a joke in this neighborhood, Luisa?" demanded Machado. "Do you know that? Lorenzo Machado has a *loco* for a son. I have a damn . . . cowboy!"

El Tigre took the abuse stoically. But he would remember this incident with Ike Clanton. Doubly so, for Clanton had hit El Tigre in the face, right before the eyes of El Tigre's own mother. When Doc, Wyatt and Bat Masterson came to town, Clanton would have a lot to answer for. El Tigre smiled thinly, thinking of that day soon to come. The second slap caught him completely by surprise.

"You think it's funny, you big *mojón*?" snarled Lorenzo Machado. "You like the idea that you make a fool of yourself and your father too, eh?" The elder Machado raised his hand again.

"¡Ay, Lorenzo!" cried Luisa Machado. "Leave the boy alone! He harms no one. He doesn't steal; he doesn't get into trouble with drugs, or fool with the girls . . . ."

"If only he *would* fool with the girls!" said Machado in disgust. "If he'd only do *anything* like a normal boy. All he wants to do is walk around the streets dressed like God-knows-what.

And with a head full of crap that he got from my own grandfather, at that!"

With the air of a man who has made an important announcement, Lorenzo turned his back on his son and sat down heavily in his plastic-covered lounge chair before the TV set. Teddy, seeing his chance, retreated down the hall to his bedroom.

"My own grandfather did this," Machado continued, as he snapped off the still blaring TV.

El Tigre watched the street below the window. His eyes were constantly on the alert for any suspicious movement. His head rested on one hand, his elbow on the window sill. The voices coming from the Machado kitchen faded . . . .

* * * * * *

"You don't talk to me that way, Marshal," said Jimmy Clanton.

Suddenly, all sound stopped in the Long Branch Saloon. The Professor at the keyboard of the tinny, upright piano became aware of the unspoken tension in the air. The sprightly tune he was playing trailed off in hesitant discord. The people seated near Clanton's table moved away nervously. They all knew that Clanton was facing off El Tigre. And everyone knew that although El Tigre never missed, there was no point staying where one could be hit by a stray bullet or a ricochet.

"I talk how I want. When I want, Clanton," lipped El Tigre thinly.

"Then prove you got the right!" cried Jimmy Clanton, going for his gun.

Some folks said later that they had seen El Tigre make his move. They were wrong. It was simply too fast for the eye to follow. In one lightning motion, the Marshal had whipped out one of his matched .45 Colts. By the time Clanton had half cleared leather, the dark muzzle of El Tigre's Colt was staring him in the face, not six inches from the end of his sweaty, pockmarked nose!

El Tigre watched in grim satisfaction as a single drop of perspiration formed at the end of that nose and splashed silently onto the green baize tabletop in front of the outlaw. Clanton was frozen in mid-draw, fearful that El Tigre would let the cocked hammer of his .45 fall. The tense silence had become almost unendurable when Clanton cried pitifully:

"All right, Marshal. Yuh got me. For God's sake, finish it!"

El Tigre smiled a thin smile that had no mirth in it. He reached his thumb over the grip of the pearl-handled pistol and rested it firmly on the spur of the Colt's hammer. With his index finger, he lightly stroked the hair trigger of his pistol. He allowed the hammer to descend gently. And with a move as fast as his draw, he reholstered his gun.

"I don't shoot defenseless men, Clanton," growled El Tigre, softly.

Jimmy Clanton folded up like a house of cards. He pitched forward across the table in front of him and buried his face in his hands, sobbing uncontrollably. The Marshal smiled again, a grimace chillier than the midnight desert wind. Then, never taking his eyes off Jimmy Clanton, he reached for the gold watch that hung on the heavy chain across his vest. His eye flickered for a millisecond as he read the hour off the ornate face of his timepiece.

"It's half past four, Clanton," El Tigre said. "I want you out of town by five. You can start leaving now."

Clanton got to his feet and slunk to the door, like the cowardly cur he was. When he reached the swinging doors of the Long Branch, he half turned, being careful to keep his hands away from his guns.

"My brother, Ike, won't take kindly toward this, Machado," he whined.

"He can tell me about that," said El Tigre ominously. "Any time he finds the guts to face me. Ike and your whole family know where to find me."

* * * * * *

"I don't believe it!" cried Lorenzo Machado from the kitchen. He had in his hand a registered letter, just arrived. "Luisa, read this."

Luisa took the registered letter from her husband's extended fingertips, across the kitchen table. Her face reflected concern for Lorenzo, whom she had never seen in such an agitated state. Teddy, attracted by the outcry, left his chair by the window and walked into the kitchen.

"Is this bad news, querido?" Luisa asked. "If it is, I don't want to read it. I should have known when we got a registered letter that something was wrong—"

"No, no!" Lorenzo insisted. "Read it!"

As Luisa began to read the letter, her face fell and she suddenly cried out:

"*¡Ay, Diós!* It is bad news! Oh, poor abuelo!"

Hearing these words, Teddy rushed forward: "What's happened? Is Grandpa Benito sick? What's wrong? Mama, tell me!"

Tears were rolling down Luisa Machado's cheeks. "Your bisabuelo died last week, Teddy," she said. "This lawyer who sent the letter, he says that Benito felt no pain. He just went to sleep one night and never woke up . . . ."

Teddy could bear no more. Tears began blurring his eyes. He knew that in a moment, he would break down and cry. Blindly, he stumbled down the hall to his bedroom. He was glad that Iris and Alicia weren't there and Rudi was out. He went silently to the wall where bisabuelo's gun and saber had hung. He ran his hand across the old, bumpy plaster and flaking paint. Then he sat down on the edge of the bed he shared with his older brother and wept until he fell asleep. When Rudi came in, a few hours later, Teddy rolled over without a word. But Rudi was excited and wanted to talk.

"Teddy, did you hear?"

"I heard. Bisabuelo is dead."

"But there's more to it than that," Rudi said excitedly. "He left a will. Papa gets everything, the lawyer says. And there's a house! Bisabuelo left Papa a house in California. Papa is talking about moving out West." Teddy sat bolt upright in bed with this disclosure. Rudi continued: "This lawyer says that Papa inherited a house in Los Angeles. In a place called Inglewood."

Teddy lay down again. "Oh. Los Angeles," he said. "I thought you meant the real West."

"Jeez, man!" said Rudi in profound exasperation. "Can't you stop being a cowboy long enough to listen? This is a three-bedroom house, with furniture and everything. It's got a lawn and trees. There's a picture of the place in the letter. This lawyer dude wants to know if he should sell it for Papa. Says it's worth about fifty thousand bucks! And dig it: This place has orange trees, Teddy. Can you imagine that? You could have all the oranges you want. For free!"

"I don't want any oranges," said Teddy moistly. "I want my bisabuelo to be alive. That's what I want." Teddy rolled over and faced the wall. "You know, Rudi?" he said to the wall, "you guys are all a bunch of damn vultures. Picking over bisabuelo's stuff."

"Up yours, kid," said Rudi, getting under the covers. "You'll grow up someday. It's a real world out there. And the Machados got themselves a real house. Unless Papa wants to sell it and stay here in Nueva York."

"You mean he might not go to California?" asked Teddy, sitting up.

"What difference should that make to you?" said Rudi casually. "Only us vultures care about that."

"Stop jiving, Rudi," Teddy said. "Are we going, or aren't we?"

"I really don't know," said Rudi, straightening up. "But I know Papa. No way he'll trust a lawyer to sell a house without him being there. The problem is Mom. She don't want to go."

"Gee, I thought Mom would like the idea."

"Why? Just because you do?" asked Rudi. "Why should she want to go? All her friends are here in Nueva York; it's all she knows. When you think about it, it makes sense. She was born here, just like us. New York is all *we* know, too."

"But you want to go, don't you, Rudi?"

"I don't know," his brother replied. "I got two weeks until I graduate from high school. I already got a job lined up driving a cab. I was thinking that if Papa took you, Mom and the girls out to California, Jack could move back in here and share the rent with me."

Teddy nodded in understanding. This was a subject rarely discussed in the Machado household. Jack Machado, the oldest brother, was living a few blocks away with a girlfriend, Shirley Ramos. Since the day Jack had moved in with Shirley, Luisa hadn't mentioned her eldest son's name. Being strict Church, Luisa was horrified by the arrangement.

For, at 19, Shirley Ramos was already the mother of a small son. And her husband was God-knows-where. Shirley had reported her husband missing, but under New York law, it would be years before she could actively seek a divorce. Jack Machado, who truly loved Shirley, wasn't about to wait years. He'd moved in with her, over Luisa's tearful protests, years ago.

"Don't you see, Teddy?" said Rudi. "If this joint out in California is already furnished, Papa can leave the stuff we got here. That way, when Shirley and Jack moved in, we'd all have bedrooms of our own. And with the Machado name still on the mailbox, we're cool with rent control, too!"

"What does Mom say?"

"Come on. What can she say? So far as she's concerned, just me and Jack will be in this place. She won't even admit that there is a Shirley Ramos and a kid," said Rudi.

"I guess you're right, Rudi."

"You *know* I'm right, kid."

After much discussion, Lorenzo Machado decided to move to California with his wife, two daughters and Teddy. The lawyer was growing impatient as weeks slipped by and no decision had been made. The main problem, Lorenzo estimated, was one of transportation. To fly, that would be the way. But there was little money in the family savings account. Both Alicia and Iris were too old to fly half-fare and the price of five airline tickets to Los Angeles was prohibitive.

There was always Greyhound, Lorenzo said, but then there was the problem of Luisa Machado's dowry. There were certain things Luisa had owned since her wedding day: a huge mirror which hung over the living room sofa, her good dishes for special occasions, a gift from her parents and her wedding dress itself, which one day would be worn by Alicia.

But most of all, Luisa had to bring her bedroom furniture. The big mahogany bed, bureau and dresser, with an elegantly carved mirror, had belonged to Luisa's mother. She would no more leave her bedroom furniture than she would the rich, ivory crucifix that hung over her bed.

"We'll ship it, then," Lorenzo said.

"And have my mirrors broken?" protested Luisa. "Never! Where I go, my furniture goes. At the same time. Or I don't go anywhere!"

"Such things can be insured, muñeca," soothed Lorenzo.

"And they will give me money when they break my possessions? What is money for my mirrors and furniture? I can't replace them."

"Are you telling me that when we have a chance to live in a real house, you won't go? All for some sticks of furniture?"

"I go where my family goes," said Luisa firmly. "It is a simple thing. But my furniture goes with me!"

It was Rudi who came up with the solution. Even Lorenzo, who did not believe in the counsel of one's children, admitted it was a good idea. For the price of airline tickets to California, Rudi pointed out, the Machados could purchase a dependable used car and rent a U-Haul trailer for Luisa's furniture. In this way, when the family arrived in California, they would have money left over, plus local transportation.

"I was rapping with my buddy at the cab company," Rudi told Lorenzo. "He's the mechanic for the whole cab fleet. He's got this 1968 Pontiac that he just finished fixing up. He was gonna use it for his own personal car, that's how good it is. An old man in Queens owned it, and always garaged it. Papa, it looks like a new car, almost."

"Then why does this mechanic want to sell such a marvelous car?" asked Lorenzo suspiciously. "Is he such a saint that he wants the Machado family to be happy?"

"He's already got a car, Papa," explained Rudi. "He was gonna sell the other one. I asked him what he'll take for the Pontiac. He'll give you a real good price, Papa."

"And when I get halfway across the country and this great car breaks down, then what?" asked Lorenzo.

"C'mon, Papa," protested Rudi. "He ain't gonna screw me. We both work at the same place. He'd never hear the end of it. At least you could go to the garage and see it."

"*Pues bien*, I will look at it," said Lorenzo. "But remember. To look is not to buy . . . ."

No one at the dinner table heard the last words Lorenzo said. Iris and Alicia had begun to carry on. They knew that Disneyland was somewhere in Los Angeles. They'd thought of nothing but the "Magic Kingdom" since the trip to California had been mentioned.

Teddy sat in his customary place at the table, opposite his father. He made no outcry, nor any show of emotion whatever. In the general commotion, no one noticed.

* * * * * *

El Tigre sat alongside the driver of the covered wagon, his Sharp's Buffalo Rifle cradled in the crook of his left arm. His keen eyes searched the horizon for any telltale cloud of dust that could mean a party of riders on horseback. Not that there were many hostile Indians in Southwestern Ohio, but you never knew. His right hand hung easily at his side, ever ready to draw his Colt. For El Tigre knew that in the savage world of the frontier, he who relaxed his vigilance often left his bones to bleach in the sun.

The womenfolk in the back of the wagon were chattering and laughing. El Tigre nodded to himself. It was just as well they were unaware of the dangers facing them, going West. They'll never know, thought El Tigre, as long as my eye is good and my hand is fast.

He glanced at the dashboard clock of the covered wagon. Six-thirty P.M. They'd been traveling since six this morning. Lorenzo, the wagon master, had insisted on an early start to beat the traffic on the trail. But soon, they would have to stop. The way the wagon master had planned the trip, they

*should soon be coming to a Wells Fargo stop or a stagecoach
station. Then the womenfolk would sleep in the cabin, while
El Tigre and the wagon master kept watch over the wagon. In
the morning, they would take turns sharing the cabin's
bathroom and shower. Then, they would be on their way
West again . . . .*

* * * * * *

"Luisa, do you think that Teddy is sick?" shouted Lorenzo.
His wife was showering in the motel bathroom.

"What?"

Lorenzo Machado opened the bathroom door, and ignoring
the clouds of steam that greeted him, he shouted again over the
roar of the water:

"I said, do you think Teddy is sick? He didn't eat anything at
all last night. And this morning, he just looked at his cereal.
I think . . ."

Luisa turned off the water and Machado found himself shout-
ing. She emerged from the bathroom, a towel wrapped around
her. She walked to the night table by the motel bed and took a
cigarette from a pack of Winstons. She lit it, and sat down on the
edge of the bed.

Lorenzo scowled at the lit cigarette in annoyance. Luisa's
smoking was a well-worried bone of contention between the two.
As Luisa explained it, smoking was her one vice. She had begun
the habit when she was in her teens and seemed powerless to
break it. As she often told Lorenzo, "If the Church can't help me
stop, you can't, either."

"Now, what's this about Teddy?" Luisa asked.

"He doesn't eat," Lorenzo replied. "He doesn't say anything
unless he's spoken to. Tell me, do you think I was wrong, not
letting him wear that stupid cowboy suit while we travel?"

"Querido, you surprise me lately," smiled Luisa. "First, you
decide to make this trip. I never expected that. Now you actually
ask me if you've done something right or wrong. Are *you* well?"

"Very amusing. Yes, I'm well. But you don't seem too concerned about your son, woman."

"Ah, that's better!" laughed Luisa. "Now that he's *my* son
again you sound more natural."

"I'm serious, 'Ñeca. He seems half alive."

"What did you expect? You know how Teddy adored the old
man. They were closer than you ever were with Benito. I think
what you see in Teddy is grief. Everyone else in this family has
been carrying on about money, the new house, the trip to Califor-

nia. But the only tears I have seen shed for Benito Machado have been mine and Teddy's."

"Are you saying that I didn't love my own grandfather?" asked Lorenzo, stiffly.

"More than that, querido. I'm saying that you didn't even *know* him. In the three years he was with us, you two never went anywhere together or did anything. Not the way he and Teddy did."

"I had a living to make," Lorenzo said. "You *do* remember my job? I had better things to do than sit around with an old man and talk about long-dead people. And a Wild West that is just as dead."

"Claro," soothed Luisa, "But all the same, Teddy did do all those things with the abuelo. He's grief stricken, is all."

Lorenzo's dark expression lightened. He regarded his wife of 22 years. After five children and years of hard work, Luisa was still as thin and girlish as when they'd first married. A damned attractive woman, he thought.

"I'm grief stricken, too," he said aloud. "For the next five days, I must sleep out in the car, with the boy. But here and now, there is a big, beautiful bed. With a more beautiful, half-dressed woman on it."

Luisa laughed and jumped to her feet. She evaded Lorenzo's grasp as she ran past him and into the bathroom, where her clothes were hanging. Lorenzo heard the bathroom lock click. Through the door, came Luisa's voice:

"Self-denial is good for the soul," she laughed. "Besides, the kids have to use the bathroom. Go call Alicia and Iris."

* * * * * *

El Tigre watched the countryside roll by. They were passing through Indiana now. Soon, they would be approaching Missouri. El Tigre let no emotion play across his features. No hostile Indian could know from his expression just how hard El Tigre's heart was beating. For he had seen the wagon master's map shortly after lunch in Indianapolis. Soon they would be in St. Louis. As that great frontiersman, Benito Machado (God rest his soul!), had often told El Tigre, "Watch for St. Louis. They call it 'The Gateway To The West.' "

El Tigre leaned forward, his eyes on the horizon. Soon he would see The Father of the Waters, the mighty Mississippi!

* * * * * *

Five

When St. Louis turned out to be just another city, Teddy was crushed. True, there was the Gateway Arch, a huge concrete arc, visible for miles. The road map said that the arch was symbolic of St. Louis' pioneer days, when the city was truly the jumping off point for the Far West.

But what Teddy had expected to see, men and women going about in frontier garb and wagons being prepared for the trek West, was nowhere to be found. St. Louis was vertical, glass and concrete: a typical Midwestern city. And when Teddy's sister Alicia remarked of the Gateway Arch, "Gee, it looks like some giant McDonalds," the boy's desolation was complete.

If it came to that, Missouri looked much like southern Illinois, which in turn, wasn't that different from Indiana and Ohio to Teddy. The major cities were large, gray and dirty. The small towns boasted an occasional Victorian structure and the same plastic, glass and chrome shopping centers Teddy had been noting since Ohio.

Alicia and Iris had grown tired of pointing out horses and cows in fields. At first, the animals had been a novelty to the city-born children. Now, they accepted the domestic animals as part of the scenery, no more worthy of notice than the occasional billboard advertising Red Man chewing tobacco. As the Pontiac, still going strong, rolled away the miles of Interstate highway, a feeling of general boredom settled in on the Machado family.

Lorenzo, who was accustomed to the ill-paved, potholed streets of Nueva York, marveled at the smooth, wide roads, and noted with satisfaction that his daily elapsed mileage on the trip was higher than he'd anticipated. He was even growing accustomed to the U-Haul trailer that obscured his rearview mirror. He hated the trailer, for he seemed incapable of parking the cumbersome appendage unless he was able to drive straight into a parking lot and drive out again without any maneuvering.

If any of the Machado family noticed that the stops made enroute were only at restaurants and motels with extra large parking lots, no one commented. Lorenzo was secretly embarrassed by this lack of driving skill. True, he had driven a truck for many years in Nueva York, but it had been a step van, a simple delivery truck. Often the places he stopped for food and lodging weren't of the best, but at least he knew he could get in and out of them.

They soon passed through Tulsa, Oklahoma, and in acquiescence to the cries for food and drink from the backseat, Lorenzo pulled into a restaurant parking lot just beyond Tulsa. The plastic sign outside advertised "Real Western B-B-Q."

The "B-B-Q" turned out to be a pre-frozen, portion-controlled, gloppy mess between two halves of a stale hamburger bun. It was topped with a reddish, syrupy fluid that soaked into the age-hardened bun and oozed out the sides when bitten into. The finishing touch was a cardboard container of cold, rubbery french fries, accompanied by a sauce cup of a greenish-white stuff, which everyone was afraid to taste.

Never the most patient of men, Lorenzo Machado began to fume. This so-called meal had not been cheap, and the Machado budget made no provision for another lunch. Lorenzo's state of mind wasn't improved by the service, which had been worse than the lunch.

They had waited patiently at a booth for nearly a half hour before a slovenly waitress would bring them so much as a glass of water and a menu. Then there had been a wait for the food ordered, as well. When the meal finally arrived, it had been indifferently served by a middle-aged, overweight woman in a sauce-spotted, once-white uniform that had perceptible yellow stains spreading from beneath the armpits.

As he choked down the near-inedible meal, it dawned on Lorenzo just why the family was receiving this treatment. He shook his head and dismissed the thought. No, it couldn't be that! When the family filed past the cashier's desk to pay the bill, Machado couldn't restrain his doubts.

"Listen, lady," he said to the cashier, who could have been the twin sister of the woman who had served them their meal, "that stuff was awful. And we waited a long time for it, too."

The cashier shoved Lorenzo's change across the counter. She put a hand to her hair, which from years of bleaching was the color and consistency of window putty with dark roots. She gave the entire family a look of profound disdain and said, "What's the matter? Ain't it good enough here for you, beaner?"

Lorenzo had no idea what the term "beaner" meant, and he had some trouble understanding the woman's heavy Oklahoman accent. But her intent was unmistakable. To make doubly sure, Lorenzo asked her to repeat her words. When the cashier responded, she spoke very loudly and slowly, as though Lorenzo were hard of hearing.

"I said that it's too good for the likes of you," she shouted. "What's the matter Mex? Don't you *hahblow* English?"

Luisa Machado saw the storm warnings written plainly across her husband's face. She quickly put her hand on her man's arm and said in Spanish: "Be careful, querido. This is a strange place, with different ways."

"These aren't different ways," replied Lorenzo in the same language. "They are very old ways. Tell me, am I to be embarrassed by this pig of a woman because I am a Latino?"

Before Luisa could say more, Lorenzo brushed her hand from his arm. He stepped so closely to the cashier's counter that his face was only inches away from the fat woman's. Lorenzo could see scores of blackheads, coated with pancake makeup that transformed the woman's face into a pink mask that ended at her chinline. His nostrils caught her sour personal scent, mingled with cheap perfume. Very elaborately and slowly, Lorenzo said in English:

"Listen to me, you foolish woman. I have eaten your bad food. I have put up with the rotten service at this pigsty. But I will be double damned if I will take insults from a sow who isn't fit to shine my wife's shoes."

Luisa herded the children out the door, fearful of the consequences of Lorenzo's outburst. As she prodded Teddy into the parking lot, she turned to see Lorenzo throw the handful of change he'd received into the cashier's face. "Here's a tip for you, *puta*!" he cried, then turning on his heel, marched indignantly to his family and car.

He jammed the gear selector of the Pontiac into "drive." Spraying the driveway with gravel from his spinning wheels, Machado pulled back onto the highway. In doing so, he nearly hit a passing car. It seemed to make him even more angry. They had gone no more than 10 miles when Lorenzo saw the police car with its flashing dome light drawing up behind him.

Machado immediately checked his speed. The speedometer needle indicated 55 miles per hour. What was this about? He'd done nothing wrong. He assumed that the police car was in pursuit of someone else, and obligingly pulled over to let the patrol cruiser go by. But it didn't pass the Pontiac. It pulled up alongside them, and a policeman in a cowboy hat motioned them to stop on the shoulder of the road.

The patrol car stopped in front of the Pontiac and its driver got out. He was a tall, redfaced man with a grotesque pot belly. As he approached the Machado car, he unsnapped the leather thong that held his service revolver in its holster.

"¡Diós Mío!" cried Luisa. "He wants to shoot us!"

"Don't be foolish, woman," snapped Lorenzo. "There must be a mistake."

But there was no mistaking the policeman's intentions. He had unholstered his pistol and was striding purposefully toward them!

"All right, you people," he drawled, "out of that car with your hands up."

In a state of shock, the Machados obeyed. The policeman had Lorenzo lean across the hood of the car. Just like on TV, Teddy thought. Having satisfied himself that the Machado family was unarmed, the policeman in the cowboy hat regarded the little group with unconcealed distaste.

"I got a report on you people," the policemen said. "Causin' a disturbance at Rose's Barbeque, and assaulting the owner. In Oklahoma we got laws against that sort of thing, Mex."

Lorenzo acted like a cartoon character getting a bright idea. He felt as though there should be a little light bulb in a balloon above his head. Perhaps there was a way out of this trouble!

"Pardon me, officer," he said. "But you have made some sort of mistake. Didn't I hear you call me Mex? Does this mean you think I am a Mexican?"

"Well, if you ain't, you're damndest bunch of Irishmen I ever did see."

Though it stung him to his soul, Lorenzo put on an affable smile and asked, "Is it all right if I lower my hands?" The redfaced policeman looked down and realized that he still held his pistol in his hand. He motioned Lorenzo to lower his hands, and then holstered his gun.

"Now look," said Lorenzo with a smile that hurt his face, "you have obviously made some sort of mistake, officer. You say you are looking for some Mexican people? We are not Mexicans. We are Puerto Ricans: Americans like yourself. My wife and children were born in New York City and I came here from Puerto Rico when I was just a boy. We are strangers to Oklahoma, only passing through on our way to California. And though it is true that we speak Spanish as well as English, we are good, respectable people on our way to Los Angeles, that's all."

The redfaced policeman looked doubtful for a second. He pushed his wide-brimmed hat onto the back of his head and surveyed the Machados and their car.

"No mistake," he drawled. "Rose said a bunch of Mexes in a Pontiac junker with New York tags. That's you, all right. And just in case you think you get out of this one, she said they was draggin' a U-Haul. If it's a coincidence, chico, it's a helluva big one!"

Lorenzo sighed deeply. There was no denying what he had done or said in that filthy restaurant. But he had seen much worse incidents in New York eating places. Considering the circumstances, Lorenzo felt he had exercised great restraint in dealing with the surly cashier at Rose's Barbeque. But this fat cop was going to arrest him. Lorenzo had little doubt of that.

A strange calm came over Machado. At this point, he thought, I have no more to lose. He glanced at the policemen's right hand, and what he saw gave him courage. Lorenzo straightened his shoulders and took a deep breath.

"I know the place you speak of, and that woman, as well," he said. "I was just there with my wife and children. After waiting there for nearly an hour, we were given a meal not fit for a pig. But I did not protest. Nor, did I speak sharply to the woman who threw the meal on the table.

"I paid my bill, and was ready to go without another word. For there are good and bad restaurants anywhere in this world. I simply thought I'd come across a bad place is all. But then this . . . woman. She tells me that I am not fit to eat the slop she serves. And worse things, she said as well."

Lorenzo spread his arms expressively, the picture of wronged innocence. Then, in a seemingly casual manner, he asked of the policeman:

"Tell me sir, have you ever been in the service?"

"Marine Corps, for four years," said the policeman in the cowboy hat. "And damned proud of it!"

"Then we have much in common," said Lorenzo. "I was a medical corpsman in the Navy. Assigned to Fleet Marines."

"I'll be damned!" said the policeman, smiling. "So was I! I was with the Second Marines. In Korea in 1951 and 1952."

"Then you understand, as a fellow Marine. In Korea, I was good enough to treat your wounded buddies on the battlefield. I was good enough to die, if need be. And as a civilian, I have never broken a law in my life. I am a hardworking man, with a family I love."

Lorenzo could tell by the redfaced policeman's expression that his remarks were not going unheeded. He pressed his case:

"So when that woman at the restaurant told me," he continued, "that I wasn't good enough to eat a crappy meal, thrown at me by a slut of a waitress, I *still* paid my bill. But when she insulted my wife and made me look like dirt in front of my children, I threw the change in her face. But assault her? I wouldn't touch her with a shovel!"

"I see. . . ." said the policeman.

"So you see, officer," Lorenzo said hurriedly. "I am guilty. I am guilty of being a good husband and father. I am guilty of working hard. I am guilty of risking my life for my country and shipmates. And worst of all, I am guilty of being a man with two huevos, who won't be humiliated by a piggish woman whose English isn't as good as mine!"

Lorenzo held out his hands to the policeman, as though awaiting handcuffs. "Now you can take me away for that," he concluded defiantly.

The redfaced policeman looked at Lorenzo, who still stood with his hands outstretched. For a long moment, the policeman was silent. Then, as though he had come to a decision, he set his cowboy hat back squarely upon his head and said:

"Excuse me, sir. I see I musta made a mistake here . . . Yep, that's it. A mistake. See, I was on the lookout for a carful of Mexicans. And you sure ain't that. You're Porto Ricans. Sorry I troubled you. Y'all have a nice trip to California, now."

The policeman turned and walked back to his patrol car. Before he opened the door, he looked back at the Machado family, still standing alongside the Pontiac. A faint smile crossed the cop's face.

"By the way," he called back to Lorenzo. "Rose *is* a little bit piggish. I don't eat there, either." Then he got into his car and rapidly disappeared down the highway.

The Machados got back into the Pontiac and drove back onto

the highway. A silence hung over the car for the first few miles of driving. Then finally, from the back of the car, Alicia made a noise like a pig grunting. The family was still laughing as they crossed the state line into Texas.

* * * * * *

El Tigre shifted his weight on the front seat of the covered wagon. They were entering Texas, which didn't look all that different from Oklahoma, when . . .

* * * * * *

"Will you look at that?" said Lorenzo Machado. He pointed to his left as the Pontiac sped down the string-straight Texas highway. Off in the distance, it seemed that the rest of the United States had somehow disappeared. One could truly see for miles and miles. Seemingly endless plains of dusty yellow green rolled off to the edge of the horizon.

"Look! Look over there!" called Iris from the backseat.

She pointed off to the right-hand side of the road. There, who could judge how far away, stood a mesa. Without reason or explanation, the huge, flat-topped mass of stone rose straight up, hundreds of feet into the air.

Perhaps it wasn't so much the sheer height of the mesa that was impressive, but the fact that no tree, building or hill broke the surface of the endless plain. The mesa seemed to soar so high as to touch the cloudless Texas sky.

"I guess this is what they mean by wide open spaces," said Luisa Machado. "It's just like a John Wayne movie."

"Look at all those cows!" cried Alicia Machado.

The family looked off to their left. Behind a barbed wire fence separating the highway from the adjoining land was a herd of white-faced cattle. Teddy quickly pointed out that they weren't longhorns.

As they watched, a plume of dust came over a slight rise in the uneventful terrain. It headed toward the herd. As it came nearer, Teddy could see the dust was caused by an open Jeep moving at a fair rate of speed over a dirt trail. Craning his neck over the back seat as the Pontiac sped by, Teddy could just barely make out the driver. He wore a cowboy hat.

Though Teddy knew from television and his great-grandfather's stories that modern cattle ranchers use men in Jeeps, rather than horsemen, seeing it done was a different matter. My first real cowboy, he thought, bitterly. And what's he riding? A Jeep! Maybe Papa is right, he thought glumly. The real West is long dead. He lapsed into silence and drifted into reverie.

The car was entering Amarillo when Teddy saw his second cowboy. This time, he wasn't disappointed. The Pontiac overtook a man on horseback, riding alongside the shoulder of the road. The car was moving slowly and Teddy got a chance to see the rider well. It almost restored Teddy's faith in Texas.

The cowboy was wearing a well-weathered Stetson, a Western shirt, high-topped cowboy boots and faded blue jeans. His face was tanned to a mahogany hue. As the car passed the horseman, Teddy caught a glimpse of pale blue eyes. The rider's eyes met Teddy's, and in that instant, the cowboy smiled and raised a hand in greeting. It made the boy's day. Now that was a real cowboy!

A few hours later in Amarillo, with dinner eaten and the family women settled in at the Western Rest Motor Inn, Teddy was bedded down in the backseat of the Pontiac. He was still awake, looking from time to time at the stars which seemed so thick in the Texas night sky. In the front seat, with pillow and blanket, was Lorenzo. He, too, was looking at the sky. But his thoughts were two thousand miles away, in Nueva York.

My God, Lorenzo thought. Here I am in Texas. I'm on my way to a place I've never seen. Driving through places I've only heard of. What got me into this? I had a good job. I only had to drive from the Bronx to Manhattan twice a day, five days a week. I had an apartment I could afford, with enough room for my family. But here I am. In Texas, of all places! What am I doing here? Lorenzo asked of himself.

He smiled when he thought of Benito Machado's words years before. So I am scared of new things in life, eh abuelo? You should see me now!

Perhaps you were right, Old Man. Now that I think about it, was I so happy in Nueva York? Or was I just used to things as they were? The dirt, the roaches, the rats? Constantly walking with your eyes on the ground to avoid dog droppings? Watching my two daughters turn into tough, street kids? (Ah, Luisa has told me of the dirty words they are picking up in the streets!)

And could Alicia and Iris ever find good hardworking husbands in Nueva York? Could I stop them, Lorenzo thought, from becoming like my son Jack's girlfriend? A fatherless child to care for; getting welfare checks? But I don't even have a job in California. What will it be like there?

"Papa? Are you asleep?"

Teddy's voice broke into Lorenzo's thoughts and startled him. He'd thought the boy had been asleep for hours. "No, hijito," Lorenzo answered. "I'm awake. What's wrong? Do you have to use the bathroom?"

"No, Papa. I'm okay. I was just thinking about the cop. The one that stopped us back in Oklahoma."

"That mojón? He's not to be thought about!" Lorenzo answered.

"I didn't mean that, Papa," Teddy said. "I meant all those battles and things. I knew you were in the Navy, but I didn't know you were a war hero."

"I wasn't," laughed Lorenzo Machado softly. "I was a machinist's mate on an aircraft carrier. The roughest it ever got for me, the ice cream machine broke down miles off the Korean coastline!"

"Then it was all lies, what you told that cop?"

"What lies?" said Lorenzo. "Yes, I was in the Navy during the Korean War. Yes, I could have been in combat. It just so happened that I wasn't. But I did notice that lump of an Oklahoma cop was wearing a Marine Corps ring.

"He seemed about the same age as I am. And I happen to know that Marines and ex-Marines are like children when it comes to talking about the Corps. If you have the time, any ex-Marine will bend your ear all day about the good old days. As this cabrón policeman was about my age, it was a safe bet he'd been in Korea. I said what I said, and he let us go."

"But Papa, wasn't it wrong to lie about being a war hero?"

"What would have been right?" asked Lorenzo angrily. "To go off to jail for that pig of a woman in the restaurant? To leave your mother and my children alone in a place like Oklahoma? I did the only smart thing to do."

Lorenzo swiveled around and faced his son. "Grow up, boy!" he said. "Use your head for something besides dreaming. Now, get to sleep. We have to get an early start tomorrow morning."

Teddy lay in the back seat, not speaking. He had been about to tell Lorenzo how proud he felt that his father had been a real war hero. Just as Benito Machado had been in 1916 and 1918. But it seemed after all, that Teddy's father was still the same man, saying the same things. . . .

* * * * * *

El Tigre walked down the center of the dusty, unpaved street. His hands hung loosely at his sides; his long, thin fingers twitching in anticipation of any sudden move from a window or doorway. This time, Clanton would realize he was

no match for El Tigre. Even if El Tigre's father wasn't really
a war hero . . . .

* * * * * *

About 11 o'clock, El Tigre drifted off to sleep. He felt nothing
when Lorenzo Machado reached across the backseat and ad-
justed the blanket that covered his son. Nor did he feel the light
touch as Lorenzo patted the sleeping boy's cheek. Machado
sighed and lay back. His thoughts were still of Nueva York and
the great adventure that lay ahead in California.

Six

It was four A.M., two days later when the Pontiac pulled up in front of the house in Inglewood. It was then that Lorenzo Machado realized he'd committed a serious oversight. In his haste to end the cross-country motor trip, he had elected to press on to Los Angeles, crossing the desert in the evening's cooler weather. And though Lorenzo knew he was at the proper address, in the right section of Los Angeles, there was one thing wrong. He didn't have the keys to the house, and wouldn't until he could see the lawyer who had written to him from California.

Machado looked into the backseat of the car. Luisa and the girls were sleeping, as was Teddy by his side. Lorenzo glanced at the dashboard clock on the Pontiac. Five hours before he could telephone the lawyer. Resigning himself to the situation, Machado made himself comfortable and settled down to sleep.

He hadn't been dozing for more than a few moments when he heard a strange noise from behind the Pontiac. He stirred, then in a flash was wide awake. Someone was trying to break into the U-Haul trailer!

He looked into the side-view mirror that came with the U-Haul setup and saw a figure behind the trailer. It was a boy, not much older than Teddy. He was holding a flashlight, covering most of the beam with his hand. Someone else, out of Lorenzo's field of vision, was worrying at the cheap lock on the trailer door.

Machado looked frantically through the clutter of the front seat for something, anything he could use as a weapon. He knew well that anyone desperate enough to break into a trailer, while its owners slept only feet away, would be armed. But search as he might, Machado could find nothing more menacing in the Pontiac's glove compartment than a toothbrush.

Lorenzo Machado had a decision to make. He could allow the thieves to proceed unhindered. But then he would have to face Luisa, and explain the loss of her belongings. Or, he might try to chase off the burglars, and risk being hurt, maybe (God forbid!) killed. Then the idea came.

As quietly as he could, Lorenzo shifted his weight and extracted the ignition keys of the car from his pocket. He slipped the key silently into the slot on the dashboard. He glanced into the side-view mirror and could no longer see the figure of the young boy.

Bueno, he thought. They're both behind the trailer now. Praying that the engine would start on the first crank, he twisted the ignition key in the lock. Praise God, the engine started with a roar.

Machado immediately jammed the car into reverse. The Pontiac lurched backwards, and Lorenzo heard a cry and a sickening thump from behind him. Then he threw the Pontiac into "drive" and floored the gas pedal. As he pulled away briskly from the house he owned, but couldn't enter, Machado again looked into his side-view mirror.

Lying on the ground was an older man, the burglar he hadn't seen. As Lorenzo watched, the boy leaned over the prostrate form of the older man. Then the kid ran off. By then, Lorenzo had turned a corner, and the two were lost to his sight.

The commotion had awakened everyone in the car. Alicia began to cry, and the inside of the Pontiac was filled with exclamations and questions from all. Machado ignored them and didn't stop driving until he came to a large, 24-hour drive-in on Century Boulevard. It had a large parking lot, and Machado knew he would have no problem with the trailer.

He pulled into the lot and switched off the ignition. He sat for five minutes, his hands shaking from the after-reaction. Finally, to his wife's persistent questioning of what had happened, he replied:

"Nothing serious, Luisa. Some people were just welcoming us to Los Angeles, that's all." He then explained fully.

The family had an early breakfast at the drive-in, then waited until they could telephone the lawyer's office. At the given time, Lorenzo spoke with the attorney, a Mr. Cepeda. He explained to the lawyer that he was unable to leave his belongings in the U-Haul for any length of time. He told Cepeda what had happened earlier.

"Then don't come here, to my office," said Cepeda. "I'll

come to you. I was going to read the will to you at my office, then turn over what I must to you. But I can't have you thinking that all Angelenos are out to rob you. Meet me at Benito Machado's house in . . . two hours. I'll bring along my secretary for a witness, and the necessary papers, okay?"

"But what about the old man I hit with the trailer?" Machado protested. "What if he's still lying there on the pavement by my house?"

"Listen to me, Señor Machado," came Cepeda's voice over the telephone. "You must understand that I am an attorney, and as such, I am an officer of the court. So, what I say is only between us."

"*Entendido* . . . understood," replied Lorenzo.

"*Bien.* Now this man that you hit. He was breaking into your property at 4 in the morning. Surely, if he were able to get up after you *accidentally* hit him, he has run off. If he was unable to get up, the people who helped him up were undoubtedly policemen. I hardly think the man would press charges. To do that, he would have to explain his actions at that hour. And that, Señor Machado, would place him squarely in jail. Do you see?"

"I see."

"Moreover," continued Cepeda, "your area is very well patrolled. It was a fluke that such an incident took place to begin with. I'm sure that a patrol car has passed through your area since 4 this morning. No, I feel you can safely meet me at Benito Machado's house without worrying. I'll see you there." The lawyer hung up.

Lorenzo returned to the table in the restaurant, where Luisa asked, "What did the lawyer say?"

"He said," Lorenzo replied smiling, "that Los Angeles is no different from Nueva York."

The small, yellow-painted stucco house sparkled in the morning sun, the early light catching the red tiles on its roof. By daylight, the neighborhood looked different. The house was situated on a side street near Century Boulevard, one of the main thoroughfares of Inglewood. Though nearly 40 years old, the little house had been well maintained. It was completely enclosed by a 4-foot-high chain link fence, behind which grew hedges, badly in need of trimming.

All the Machados, save Lorenzo, spent the time waiting for the lawyer to arrive by exploring the grounds and peering through the windows of the locked house. As the letter from Cepeda had said, the interior was fully furnished. As advertised, there were two orange trees in back, flanked by a sickly looking avocado tree. While the rest of the family oohed and aahed over each new discovery, Lorenzo doggedly continued to unload the U-Haul trailer onto the front lawn of the little house.

In the darkness, hours before, Lorenzo hadn't noticed that there was also a driveway and a small garage. Had the driveway gate been unlocked the night before, Lorenzo mused, the incident with the two thieves wouldn't have happened at all.

Machado had been somewhat apprehensive when he'd returned to the place. He'd half expected to see police gathered, or perhaps even the body of the old man. He walked over to the spot where the incident had taken place. There were no bloodstains on the street. Relieved, he continued unloading the trailer.

The attorney arrived a half hour late. He pulled up in front of the Machado house driving a Mercedes-Benz sports car. He came around to the passenger side of the car and opened the door, allowing a strikingly beautiful young woman to exit.

Cepeda was a short, stocky, balding man, dressed in a butter-colored suit which Lorenzo correctly guessed was made of raw silk. The exquisite woman, who Cepeda introduced as "Miss Vega, my secretary," was as elegantly turned out as Cepeda. She wore a white linen suit.

Miss Vega didn't appear to notice how carefully she was being scrutinized by Luisa Machado as she followed Cepeda up to the porch of the little house. Luisa also noticed how carefully Lorenzo was observing Miss Vega's well-clad form. Luisa gave Lorenzo a sharp dig in the ribs with her elbow.

"Keep your eyes to yourself, Machado," she hissed.

"¡Querida!" whispered Lorenzo, his face a mask of pure innocence. "This is business!"

"I know your business, Machado," gritted Luisa. "And you don't need any secretary on your truck."

"Oh, come on Ñeca," said Lorenzo. "Let's hear the will read."

"Fine with me," Luisa replied. "The sooner that woman is out of my house, the better."

The lawyer produced a key ring and opened the front door. All the Machados filed in after him and Miss Vega.

Thirty minutes later, Lorenzo sat in the living room, stunned. He had just heard aloud the last written words of his grandfather. The language of the will was couched in legal terms, unfamiliar to

Machado. But through it all, there was no mistaking the intent and iron resolution of the late Benito Machado.

The little house, fully paid for, the land beneath it, the furniture inside it . . . all were left to Lorenzo Machado. And after taxes and Cepeda's legal fees were paid, there was even $6,000 left over! All the distant cousins who may have expected to share in Benito Machado's legacy were to be disappointed. With one exception, everything had been willed to Lorenzo Machado.

"Señor Cepeda," Lorenzo asked, "will you kindly read me the part about my son again?"

"Surely, señor," smiled Cepeda. "Actually, the boy should be present. He *is* mentioned in this will."

Teddy, who had been exploring the new house with Alicia and Iris, was brought into the living room and introduced to the lawyer. "Young man," Cepeda said, "you are a very fortunate person. Your bisabuelo has left you some important effects and a small amount of cash."

Teddy dug his toe into the carpet of the Machado's new living room. He was unaccustomed to carpeting in private dwellings. Movie houses were different. In fact, Teddy had often wondered what sort of linoleum rich people had on their floors. When Luisa saw what Teddy was doing to the carpet, she leaned over and pinched his forearm.

"Leave the rug alone!" she snapped.

Teddy returned his attention to Cepeda and Miss Vega, seated on the sofa. "I don't care about the will," he said. "I don't want anything."

"Now, now, young man," Cepeda said easily. "That's no way to think. Your great-grandfather was kind enough to mention you in his will. The least you can do is listen."

"I told you," Teddy protested. "I don't want anything. If I could have what I wanted most, I'd want bisabuelo alive again."

"The boy and my grandfather were very close," explained Lorenzo to the lawyer.

"I see," said Cepeda.

Then in that tone adults who despise children employ when speaking to them, Cepeda asked of Teddy: "Listen, young man. If your bisabuelo had given you a present while he was still alive, would you have taken it?"

"Yes, he gave me presents before."

"Good. You understand then. Well, my boy, a will is just a piece of paper, like a letter from Beyond. This paper says, 'Even though I am gone, I want my great-grandson to have a present from me.'

"Now, my boy, would you turn down this last present, and hurt the feelings of your bisabuelo in heaven?"

"No, I . . . guess not."

"Bueno. That is good," said Cepeda, twirling the heavy gold and diamond ring he wore on his pinky finger. "For your bisabuelo wanted you to have some things of his, and some cash money. You *must* take them, or it's an insult to your great-grandfather's memory. And you wouldn't want that, would you?"

"No. . . ."

"Very well, then. I shall read to you your bisabuelo's exact words. Remember. This is he, speaking to you from beyond the grave. And he is speaking only to you. This will reads":

To my great-grandson, Teodoro Machado, I bequeath the sum of $500. This money is not to be placed in trust, nor deposited in a bank. It is to be given to the boy, to spend as he sees fit. It is my hope that he will use it to have one hell of a good time.

I also leave to my great-grandson, my Colt .45 pistol, gunbelt, holster and U.S. Cavalry saber. He is also to receive my three Stetson hats and four pairs of dress boots, to be worn at such time as he grows to fit them.

While I am aware that there is some danger in bequeathing a pistol to an adolescent boy, I also know that my great-grandson is no ordinary lad. I have lectured him long and well on the proper and safe use of firearms. Yet, before the pistol is turned over to him, a portion of the money I have left to Lorenzo Machado, my grandson, must be used to have Teddy instructed by a professional as to the pistol's proper use and maintenance. . . .

Teddy stood, as though rooted to the carpet of the living room. Bisabuelo's pistol and saber! Teddy had thought that his great-grandfather would surely have been buried with these things. And Benito Machado's hats and boots! The cash couldn't have meant less to Teddy. Once Cepeda had mentioned Benito

Machado's effects, Teddy was in a different world. . . .

* * * * * *

El Tigre stood at the graveside as the last shovel of earth was patted down by Mr. Smiley, the town undertaker. The grim-faced lawman read once more the simple epitaph on the wooden grave marker:

★ BENITO MACHADO ★
1889-1979
Un Hombre de Honor

A man of honor. That was it, El Tigre thought.

The weight of the Colt .45 bequeathed to him by the old man was heavy on his hip. El Tigre swore at that moment that the Colt would never be drawn and fired, save in the cause of Justice and Fair Play.

If Smiley the undertaker noted the single tear that slowly ran down El Tigre's cheek, he didn't mention it. Few men would dare. . . .

* * * * * *

"Teddy! Didn't you hear what Mr. Cepeda said?" Luisa Machado asked. "Don't you know how to thank him?"

"I need not be thanked, Señora Machado," said Cepeda, pushing both hands before him, as though declining an extra dessert. "The gift came from Benito Machado. I serve as a mere messenger after my client's death."

Cepeda consulted a gold watch he wore on his left wrist. He was obviously anxious to leave. Then, to Lorenzo, he said:

"I can see that the boy is still upset. If you can have him leave the room, there are a few other matters which I feel we should discuss."

"Of course," said Lorenzo, and turning to Teddy he said, "hijito, go see what your sisters are doing. And tell them not to open any closet doors unless your mama is with them."

Teddy went off in search of Alicia and Iris, and the Machados were once again alone with Cepeda and his secretary. The attorney glanced toward the living room door, as though to make sure they were not heard.

"Obviously, one does not turn over a deadly weapon to a mere boy," the lawyer said, smiling. "If you feel it truly important that the boy has this pistol, I would advise you to take the gun to a shop and have it rendered harmless. The firing pin could be filed off and the barrel filled with melted lead.

"In this way, the boy can have his toy, and can do no more harm than he would with a capgun. And you will not worry about a dangerous piece of hardware like this lying about the house. Understood?"

"Entendido," replied Lorenzo Machado. "But won't this process you speak of also destroy the value of the gun? I have heard that old pistols can be quite valuable."

"Valuable to whom?" inquired Cepeda, lifting his eyebrows. "The boy has no earthly use for an antique pistol. It's a dangerous, deadly thing. And if he receives the instruction that Benito Machado's will calls for, even Teddy will learn that I am right in this matter."

"I doubt that," Luisa Machado said. "The boy lives in a fantasy world of cowboys."

"That may be," said Cepeda, dismissing Luisa's objection with an airy wave of his jeweled hand. "But a gun is a gun. It is dangerous. I would also suggest that you have the edge of that saber blunted on a grinding wheel."

Cepeda reached into the inside pocket of his elegant suit and produced a gold cigarette case. He proffered the opened case to Lorenzo and Luisa. Luisa accepted a cigarette, Lorenzo declined. The attorney lit the cigarettes with a heavy gold lighter.

"You understand, Señor Machado," he continued, "I am torn between my responsibility to my late client and my obligations as an officer of the court. I have therefore decided that before I can turn this gun and saber over to the boy, that these things of which I spoke must be done."

"My God!" exclaimed Lorenzo Machado. "Do you think for a moment that I want these things around the house?

"I quarreled seriously with my grandfather about this very subject. He had filled Teddy's head with so much of this cowboy crap that the boy was nearly thrown out of school.

"If it were up to me, I'd throw the damned things into the East River!"

"That's quite a long way to throw, Señor Machado," smiled Cepeda.

"Then the damned Pacific Ocean. You know what I mean!"

"Yes, I do know what you mean, señor," said the attorney. "Nevertheless, the will is quite specific. I am bound to follow its instructions. Handle it as I have told you. With these dangerous gifts made harmless, I can satisfy both the terms of the will and common sense."

Cepeda stood up. "I will have your check for $6,000 drawn and put into the mail today. You will receive final title to this house through the court in a few months' time. There will be a separate check for Teddy's $500."

Lorenzo got to his feet and took the lawyer's extended hand. With Miss Vega behind them, they walked to the small front porch of the house. As he was about to leave, Cepeda said quietly to Lorenzo.

"I noticed when I arrived that there were no dead bodies of thieves laying about.

"You see how needlessly you worried? And in the same way, you must listen to me about this gun and sword affair. Once you have lead poured down its barrel, the gun will be harmless. The sword is another matter. Even with a blunted edge, it still has a point. I wouldn't allow Teddy to play with that. Hang it on a wall."

"I shall," Lorenzo replied. "But tell me, where does one have this melted lead business done to the pistol?"

"Any gun shop can do it," Cepeda said. "There are several reputable shops in this area."

"¡Diós mío!" cried Lorenzo. "Do you mean to tell me that in Los Angeles, one may buy a gun at a store, like a loaf of bread?" Machado was thinking of the strict handgun laws in New York City.

"I'm afraid it *is* that easy," replied Cepeda, grimly, then added, "and in 1968, Senator Robert Kennedy was not shot by a loaf of bread. I feel it is much too easy to buy a gun in Los Angeles, señor."

"If it's that easy, you must be a busy lawyer," said Lorenzo.

"I do not practice criminal law, señor," said Cepeda coolly. He again shook hands with Lorenzo and gave a short bow to Luisa. Then he and Miss Vega departed in the Mercedes-Benz.

Lorenzo put his hand on his wife's shoulder as they walked back into the house. "Muñeca," Lorenzo said, "I know that we have just come into money. More money than we have ever had. I also know that Cepeda is a wealthy lawyer and seems to be a man of honor. . . ."

"Then what troubles you, querido?" asked Luisa.

"I don't know," replied Lorenzo. "But somehow, some way in which I don't understand, I think we've been screwed by this fancy lawyer."

"Aha!" crowed Luisa. "If I had kept still and let you keep your eyes nailed to that fancy secretary," she said, dripping scorn upon the word secretary, "you wouldn't have noticed anything. Just her expensive butt," she laughed.

"But I know what you mean. I too, feel we have been diddled by this man with all his gold jewelry."

"But how? In what way?" Lorenzo asked.

Luisa smiled and shrugged her shoulders. "All I know is that every time a lawyer deals with a working man, the working man always gets a screwing. That's what lawyers are about, querido."

"I suppose," said Lorenzo. "But I believe he is right about making the pistol and saber harmless. I will look into this matter tomorrow."

Teddy stood unmoving, his body pressed flat against the wall of the kitchen alcove that adjoined the living room. He had heard all the conversation between Machado and Cepeda. . . .

* * * * * *

They would never spike El Tigre's pistol. It didn't matter what the lawyer and Clanton had said. Somehow, El Tigre would outsmart them all. He feared them not. The forces of injustice and evil had been trying to kill El Tigre for years. And so far, he was still alive. . . .

* * * * * *

Seven

The next five days at the little house in Inglewood were hectic. At the heart of a whirlwind made up of mops, buckets and paper towels, Luisa Machado was making the new house her own. No one else's idea of clean was clean enough for Luisa. At times the heady smell of pine-scented cleaning liquid was so strong that Lorenzo Machado would carry a chair from the kitchen to the front porch. There, free from vapors, he would watch the traffic passing by on the street.

It gave Lorenzo great satisfaction that only an occasional car or truck drove past the little house. In Nueva York, such peace and quiet came only during the hours of 3 and 5 in the morning.

Lorenzo had also discovered a nearby Spanish grocery that carried the same brand of beer he had drunk in New York, Schaefer's. To Lorenzo it was like a bit of Nueva York in California to sip from the familiarly labeled can.

But Machado's inner happiness sprang from another source, the California climate. It was more homelike here to Lorenzo than Nueva York had been. It stirred near-forgotten memories of his young boyhood in Ponce, Puerto Rico.

Further nostalgia came from an apartment building across the street. It had been many years since Lorenzo had seen a palm tree. His thoughts went drifting back to what Benito Machado had said three years ago when they had parted company in Nueva York.

The old man had said that Lorenzo would never own the little house or small business he'd dreamed of most of his life. It was ironic, Lorenzo mused, that in order for the dream to come true, the old man had to die.

Benito Machado would never see Lorenzo sitting on his own front porch, sipping Schaefer. Lorenzo smiled to himself. As he looked again up the street, his smile disappeared. Down the block walked his son, dressed in that absurd cowboy suit!

Teddy cut a figure comical to anyone but his father. The western outfit his bisabuelo had given him years ago was long outgrown. His arms protruded fully three inches from the cuffs of his shirt. Teddy's gait was awkward, as his boots no longer fit. The bottoms of his frayed black whipcord trousers hovered above his ankles.

But if his finery was tarnished, it meant nothing to Teddy Machado. He walked in a world completely his own, oblivious to the three small neighborhood children who followed paces behind him. They were calling out names in Spanish and English. Lorenzo winced as he heard the words loco, Marshal Dillon, and worse.

Oh God! he thought, is this to begin again, here in California? Was the name of Machado again to be a neighborhood joke? No, by God, Lorenzo swore! He would have words with his son. After dinner, perhaps.

He thought briefly of Benito Machado's pistol and saber, hidden in a place where Teddy could not find them. Lorenzo had been meaning to go to one of the gun stores the lawyer Cepeda had mentioned. But somehow, the errand hadn't been done.

I must have that damned gun fixed, Lorenzo thought. Look at that boy! He looks like a cowboy's idea of a scarecrow!

* * * * * *

El Tigre walked in silence, ignoring the jeers and cat-calls from the townspeople. They were, after all, of no consequence. El Tigre had more important things on his mind. Soon the Colt .45, his personal weapon, would be in his hands. In the meantime, he would act as though the two toy pistols at his side were real ones.

It didn't matter what the townies said or did. He felt just like Jimmy Stewart in Destry Rides Again. *That's all right, he thought. I'll take their abuse and laughter. A strong man needs no company other than his own. And soon, my day will come. When I strap on bisabuelo's Colt. Then Ike Clanton, watch out!*

* * * * * *

Lorenzo Machado fled the porch before Teddy turned in at the gate. It was enough the boy was called loco and ridiculed by the neighborhood kids. But Lorenzo couldn't bear to hear and see it done.

What did I do wrong? he thought. The boy was fine all the way across country on the drive. Quiet, it's true, but he was no problem.

And look at where we live now, Machado thought. Teddy has his own bed and room. The girls have theirs. I hoped he would stop this cowboy crap once we got out here. But then the old man had to leave him that pistol!

It seems that Benito is having the last laugh, after all. I can sit here on the porch of a house I never could have bought, and say he was wrong. But damn him, the old bastard is winning again, and from beyond the grave!

Machado walked into the kitchen and tossed the empty beer can into the trash pail. Luisa looked up from the stove, where she was preparing dinner. She smiled widely and said, "Well, Machado, have you decided? Do we go tomorrow? I can hardly wait to see the girls' faces when you tell them."

"Tell them what?" asked Lorenzo, his mind still distracted by thoughts of his poor, simpleton son.

"About Disneyland, querido," said Luisa. "You said that when the check from the lawyer arrived, we would go. Well, the check came with Teddy's parcel yesterday. The money is now in the bank. Do we go tomorrow, or not?"

"Go where, Mama?" asked Teddy, entering the kitchen.

"Ask your Papa," said Luisa, her face anticipating Teddy's reaction.

Teddy looked bewildered. "Where are we going, Papa?" he asked. "I like it here in California. Are we going back to Nueva York?"

"No son, we are staying here," Lorenzo replied. "That is, if I can find a good job. We all like it here. Your mama and I were speaking of something else. I told her that when the check from the lawyer came, we could maybe go to *Disneyland*. . . ."

"Disneyland!" squealed Alicia Machado. Attracted by the aroma of dinner cooking, and that mysterious inner clock that draws young people to the kitchen at exactly the right time every day, she had overheard the last words of the conversation. She ran across the kitchen and leaped into her father's arms.

"Oh, Papa!" she cried, "you're the wonderfulest Papa in the whole world!"

"Am I, muñeca?" Lorenzo said, holding her close. "Am I really?"

"Oh yes, Papa. Even better than that. You're more wonderful than Mick Jagger!"

Lorenzo Machado laughed loudly and gently set his daughter down.

"Is it possible that anyone can be that wonderful?" he asked. "Now that you and Iris have a room of your own, I cannot see the walls of it. There are so many pictures of this Jagger on them."

"Mick Jagger never said he'd take me to Disneyland," said Alicia with perfect logic. Then she darted out the kitchen door to the backyard where her sister waited. "Iris!" she cried. "We're going to Disneyland!"

Lorenzo sat down at the kitchen table, looked at Luisa and grinned.

"I suppose that settles it," he said. "We will go to Disneyland tomorrow. If I can find it on my road map. . . ."

"I will never find this place," groaned Lorenzo Machado. "For two whole hours, I have driven near it, past it and around it. If this next turnoff doesn't take us to an entrance, I am going back home!"

A chorus of protests arose from the backseat of the Pontiac. Both Alicia and Iris seemed close to tears. But Lorenzo was adamant. Accustomed to driving in New York, the high speed driving and wide boulevards of Southern California had thoroughly intimidated him. On two occasions, Machado had driven directly past, and in full view of, the famous amusement park. In both instances, he'd found himself in the wrong lane for a turnoff, or there was no turnoff.

The day was clear and hot. As it grew older, the temperature rose in direct proportion to Lorenzo's ire. Never a man of great restraint, Machado was dangerously close to his boiling point. Luisa knew the signs well, and hushed her two daughters. Teddy as ever, was silent. He gazed out the window, lost in his own thoughts. . . .

* * * * * *

"Think we'll ever find 'er, marshal?" asked the whiskey salesman seated opposite him in the hot, dusty stagecoach.

"We will," said El Tigre, smiling thinly. "You city fellows aren't used to the long distances out West."

"But what about Indians?" asked a lady passenger.

"There aren't any hostiles in this part of the country, ma'am," said El Tigre. "Once in a while, a bandit tries his luck at holding up a stagecoach. But that's about it."

"That's about it?" shrilled the lady passenger. "Bandits! We could all be killed. Or worse!"

"There's nothing worse than getting killed, ma'am," said El Tigre shortly, and resumed scanning the horizon.

The whiskey salesman leaned over in his seat and spoke softly to the nervous woman. As he did so, she recoiled from his breath. Evidently, the whiskey salesman was one of his own best customers. If the salesman noticed the woman's reaction to this breath, he didn't acknowledge it.

"Not to worry about bandits, ma'am," he chuckled. "That fella there's the marshal. He can handle anything that comes along."

"But he's only one man," protested the lady passenger. "Suppose there are lots of bandits?"

"You're new to these parts, ma'am," smiled the whiskey salesman, hooking a thumb over his shoulder. "That there fella is El Tigre, marshal of Dodge City and the fastest man with a gun in the whole West. You're safer in this stagecoach then in your mama's arms."

If El Tigre heard the words of praise, and his sharp ears missed nothing, he gave no sign. His craggy face was turned outward, searching the horizon. He observed with some distress, a sign that read: Disneyland.

* * * * * *

"There it is! There it is!" cried Alicia Machado. "Quick, Papa. Turn in here!"

Lorenzo wrenched on the steering wheel and nearly cut off a small car behind him. The angry toot-toot of the small car's horn annoyed Lorenzo, like the buzzing of some insect pest. Machado managed to turn the Pontiac into the driveway his daughter had noticed. Then he read the rest of the sign marked "Disneyland: Employees Only."

Machado stopped the car in the driveway. He was beyond words, beyond endurance. As he sat in furious silence, he felt his perspiration-soaked shirt clinging to his back and the vinyl upholstery. Finally, he regained control of himself and began to back out of the driveway. As he did so, a huge tractor trailer rig roared by, only inches from the rear bumper of the Machado car. Its air horn rattled the passengers of the Pontiac as it passed. Lorenzo jammed the brake pedal so hard that the car stalled. It would not restart.

"Papa . . ." Alicia began from the backseat.

"Not a word," said Lorenzo Machado through clenched teeth. "If anyone says a word, one word . . . With God as my witness it will be the last word they say!"

The engine finally caught with a bass growl, and a huge cloud of black smoke issued from the tailpipe of the Pontiac.

Machado backed out of the driveway safely and then shoved the gear selector into "drive." The old sedan lurched forward like a dowager goosed by a cattle prod. The car sped past the next gate, a hundred yards away from the employee's entrance.

The sign read, "Disneyland: Main Entrance," but Machado was going too fast to stop. With his hands gripping the wheel so tightly that his knuckles shone white, Lorenzo growled to all in the car, "Not a word. Not a damned word!"

Technically, his advice was followed to the letter. Alicia Machado didn't say a word. Instead she began to emit a long wailing cry. Ignoring all protests, Lorenzo drove on.

By the time Lorenzo had stopped for a traffic light, he had already regretted his actions. The entire purpose of this family outing had been to have a good time. It was becoming a nightmare, instead. And he *had* promised the girls this holiday.

But now, it had become a matter of pride, of *amor própio*. He would not turn back and try again to enter this amusement park. Not after he had declared his intention of returning to Los Angeles. Another traffic light loomed up and Machado cut the wheels sharply to the right.

Completely disoriented by the many turns he had made, Lorenzo wasn't quite sure in which direction he was headed. Then he spotted a sign that read: "To Los Angeles." As he drove toward the sign, the cries of protest began again from the back of the car. Luisa quickly quieted Alicia. The family rode in silence for about a mile. (Once the crying had stopped, Lorenzo again felt remorse.)

But I'll be damned if I'll turn back, he thought. It was then he saw the big billboard reading: "Knott's Berry Farm, Where the West Turns Wild!" On an impulse, he turned into the parking entrance. Lorenzo had never heard of this place. But it appeared to be some sort of amusement park, like the now-hated Disneyland, but smaller and less elaborate.

The gloom and wailing evaporated quickly as Lorenzo swung the car past a replica of Independence Hall and into the main parking lot. The park straddled a main highway, and just across the road were visible the tops of various amusement park thrill rides, the roof of a Mexican Village, and here, Teddy's heart leaped, a replica of a complete frontier town! As Lorenzo pulled into an empty parking slot, Teddy could see a man in full cowboy regalia, walking across the road opposite.

For Teddy, Knott's was a dream come true. Though Alicia and Iris oohed and aahed over each new ride, exhibit or shop, all was less then nothing to Teddy. He had eyes only for the western village reproduction. For here there were cowboys, *real* cowboys, wearing traditional costume. And actually carrying six-guns!

Teddy bitterly regretted that he wasn't wearing his own cowboy outfit. Here he could wear it and not seem out of place. If he were to draw any glances here they would be of admiration, not derision. For this was a place that understood cowboys! He was raptly watching two cowboys who were sitting on the front porch of an old-fashioned hotel, when suddenly, two shots rang out! The sudden, loud reports startled the Machado family.

"What the hell was that?" asked Lorenzo, not expecting an answer. But Teddy quickly replied:

"Six-guns, Papa. They make a really loud noise."

"¡Ay, Diós!" cried Luisa. "Can it be a holdup?" Another series of shots were heard.

"Look! Look up there on the roof!" called Alicia Machado.

The family gazed in the direction of the roof of the old-time hotel. There, atop the Ghost Town Hotel, stood a man in western garb. He was firing his pistol at a man on the ground, who was similarly dressed, a smoking six-gun in his hand.

As the family watched, wide-eyed, a mini-drama began to unfold. One of the actors (for the Machados now realized that this was staged for the amusement of the Knott's patrons) called down insults to the actor portraying the town marshal, who had gone inside the "hotel."

"Hey marshal!" called the desperado on the roof. "You scared to come out?"

Teddy noted that the man on the roof couldn't see the marshal, either. He thought back on what Benito Machado had told him about dealing with desperados . . . .

* * * * * *

El Tigre stood silently below the overhang of the hotel porch. Ignoring the taunts of Jimmy Clanton from the roof directly above, he quickly fitted two shells into his double-barreled shotgun. He clicked the breech shut and thumbed back the hammers of the "gun that can see in the dark" to full cock position. Then, with a casual grace, he removed his broad-brimmed Stetson from his head and scaled it into the street. As he did so, he moved with a catlike grace from the shelter of the overhanging porch.

Sure enough, distracted by the sudden movement, Jimmy Clanton fired at the marshal's hat. It was the split-second that El Tigre needed. Like blasts from a small artillery piece, the shotgun spoke its twin messages of hot lead and death!

Clanton reeled from the impact of the double blast. He dropped his pistol and for a sickly second, he seesawed back and forth on the edge of the hotel roof. Then slowly, he fell forward, crashing first to the roof of the hotel porch, then finally, rolling off to the street below. He landed and lay still. But Clanton was still alive when El Tigre reached his side, six-gun at the ready.

"Yuh got me fair and square, Marshal," gasped Clanton. "But this ain't the end of it. My brothers will be a-lookin' fer yuh."

El Tigre knew that in a moment, he would be speaking to a dead man. But he had enough time to say, "Clanton, if trouble comes lookin' for me, I won't be hard to find." Then he turned on his heel and strode purposefully toward Smiley's undertaking parlor.

Can't leave that body out there in the street, he thought.

From the corner of his eye, El Tigre noticed Ed Cassidy, one of the Clanton hired hands. Cassidy quickly mounted his horse and headed out of town, toward the Clanton ranch. El Tigre estimated that he had about three hours' time before Cassidy alerted the Clantons and the whole clan returned to town to seek revenge. Well, El Tigre was ready. El Tigre was always ready. . . .

* * * * * *

The amusement park P.A. system intruded on Teddy's world. "Ladies and gentlemen," came the voice over the loudspeakers, "Welcome to Knott's Berry Farm! In just 30 minutes, the World's Champion Fast Draw competition will begin at our Roaring Twenties Pavilion. If you want to see the fastest guns in the West, male and female, just go to the Roaring Twenties Pavilion. This event is being covered by national television for an upcoming special on MBC-TV. So, if you want a good view of all the shooters, be there early!"

The last echo of the P.A. system announcement hadn't died away before Teddy was headed for the section of the park called the Roaring Twenties Pavilion. The family had walked through that section earlier, and Teddy knew the location. As the boy walked by, his father grabbed him by the neck of his shirt.

"Where do you think you're going, boy?" asked Lorenzo of his son.

"To see the Fast Draw, Papa."

"I see," said Lorenzo. "And did you bother to ask if anyone else wants to see this cowboy business?"

"I do! I do!" cried Alicia Machado. Lorenzo looked askance at Luisa, who smiled and said, "It can't hurt, querido. It *is* fun when you get used to the dreadful noise these six-shooters make."

"Oh, all right," said Lorenzo grudgingly, "but if . . ."

Before Lorenzo could utter another word, Teddy was already dashing toward the Roaring Twenties Pavilion. When he reached the designated area, he found a TV crew already setting up for the show. A man was unwinding a serpent's nest of black cables, and another was testing out brilliant lights on adjustable metal stands.

Standing off to one side, with a crowd of people about him, was a man Teddy recognized. It was David Hoar, the Englishman. His TV interviews and special shows were known all over the world. Teddy noted with satisfaction that Hoar was a short man.

Under the heavy, orangey makeup the man wore, Teddy could see Hoar was much older than he appeared to be on television. The Englishman was facing a camera and speaking into a microphone. Teddy edged closer to the barrier erected by the TV crew and listened hard to make out what Hoar was saying.

"Well, here we are at Knott's Berry Farm," said Hoar. "A truly super place. Today, we are going to see a demonstration of Fast Draw by the fastest guns in the West. The speediest six-shooters in the Occident, if you will. For instance, I have here with me, the record holder and officially recognized Fastest Draw in the entire world! Here he is now, a truly super gentleman, Mr. Albert Molina, Jr. Let's give him a super hand, folks!"

Teddy nearly sank through the pavement in shock. Striding into camera range was a young man, dressed in an outfit almost identical to the one worn by Teddy's bisabuelo! Except that this man's hat brim was curled up at the edges, he could have stepped right out of the pages of Benito Machado's battered old photo album.

Teddy was immediately struck by the fact that the champion appeared not much older than he. And this was no suntanned, blue-eyed cowboy, either. Alberto Molina was a shade under 6 feet tall, and of medium olive complexion.

But Molina was lean, and he moved with the easy grace that characterizes all professional athletes. And yes, he was darkly handsome. The six-gun at his waist was shiny chrome plated, and the motif of white metal continued in his costume, with elaborately worked silver *conchos* on his black leather gunbelt.

The slim legs of his frontier suit were further adorned with silver threaded embroidery, and the sun caught the silver concho band that encircled the crown of his Stetson hat. His boots were silver chased as well. His hands hung at his sides loosely. Hands that were long and graceful, ready to fly into action.

In all, Alberto Molina was the very image of an old-time Western gunfighter. And impressive though his costume was, it was not this that made Teddy stare in wonderment. For, there was no doubt that this handsome man, the fastest man with a six-shooter in the whole world, was a Latino, just like Teodoro Ramon Machado!

Eight

Though Teddy was near-awed by Alberto Molina, the Englishman seemed to think being Fast Draw Champion of the world was some sort of joke. He was interviewing Molina as though he were a freak or a clown. Teddy was not amused by Hoar's attitude.

"So tell me, Mr. Molina," Hoar said. "Or may I call you Alberto?"

"Al is just fine," said The Champion. "Everyone calls me Al."

"Well, so shall I, then," said Hoar. "In point of fact, the fastest gun in the world can be called whatever he wants. Heh-heh-heh. Tell me Al, how did you get to be the fastest gun?"

"About 5,000 hours of practice, Mr. Hoar," replied The Champion laconically.

Teddy smiled to himself. Obviously, The Champion was no man to run off at the mouth on a TV interview. Hoar should have known. Unabashed by The Champion's reply, the fatuous Englishman pressed on.

"Well of course," he said, "that's how one gets to Carnegie Hall. Practice. But what I mean is, is there anything in your background that would lead you to this championship? What do you do for a living, Al?"

"I'm an insurance salesman, Mr. Hoar. In Los Angeles."

"Well, I'd certainly buy anything you were selling. Heh-heh-heh. You don't wear your six-shooter when you sell insurance, do you?"

"I *wear* my gunbelt and *carry* my *pistol* only when I am shooting, Mr. Hoar," corrected The Champion.

"Um . . . ah yes, I see," said Hoar, perhaps realizing that

humor was not called for. He became more serious and asked, "Now would you mind telling our audience what we will be seeing this afternoon?"

David Hoar didn't wait for a reply from Al Molina, Jr. He looked directly at the TV camera and said "Cut!" Then he turned to Al Molina and said:

"Now, you just reply to my question when the man over there points a finger at you. On this part of the show, the camera will show you approaching the targets over there and firing. But your explanation about what you are doing will be heard voice-over. Do you know what voice-over is, Al?"

"Yes, I've been on TV before," said The Champion.

Good for you, Champ! thought Teddy.

"Super!" said David Hoar. "Just say it all into the microphone. I'll be back in half a shake."

While The Champion spoke into the microphone, Hoar went over and began speaking animatedly with a man who wore a T-shirt labeled "I am the Director, I think." The conversation was long, and Teddy saw that The Champion was finished speaking into the mike. The boy saw his chance and went over to the railing separating the crowds from the TV equipment.

"Mr. Molina," Teddy called. The Champion turned and looked around.

"Over here, over here!" Teddy called again.

The Champion walked over to the railing where Teddy stood. The boy was glad that his parents and sisters, bored by the long waits between taping, had wandered off. The Champion had a small smile on his lips. Maybe, Teddy thought, a private joke was amusing The Champion.

"Yes, what can I do for you?" he asked.

For a moment Teddy was too awed to speak. Then he swallowed hard and blurted out: "You can tell me how I can be just like you!"

"For God's sake, why?" laughed The Champion. "What's wrong with being who *you* are?" Then noting the intense expression on Teddy's face, Al Molina added, "Hey, you're serious, aren't you?"

"I am, Mr. Molina. More than anything. I even got a gun and a belt and a holster. It's a real gun. A Colt .45 that my bisabuelo gave me."

"*¿Ah, tu eres un Latino, eh?*" said The Champion. "You're a Latin! I thought so. And then when you said bisabuelo, I was sure. Where are you from, er . . . ?"

"Machado. Teddy Machado," said the boy quickly. Then on an impulse he added, "But my friends call me El Tigre."

"Do they now?" said Al Molina grinning broadly. "And why do they do that, Tiger?"

"Cause I picked out the name," said Teddy. "My bisabuelo told me about this gunfighter in Texas who was called El Tigre. He wore an all-black outfit, like my bisabuelo bought for me. And this El Tigre was fast!" Teddy hesitated and quickly added, "Not as fast as you, I mean."

"I know what you mean, Tiger," smiled The Champion. "Your bisabuelo sounds like quite a man. Is he here with you, today?"

"No," said Teddy, his face clouding. "He died two months ago."

"Oh, I'm sorry," said Al Molina. "But he must have been quite old if he remembered Miguel Chacon, though."

"Remembered who?" gulped Teddy.

"Miguel Chacon," said The Champion. "He was one of the most feared and fastest men in the Old West. He had a lot of nicknames. El Tigre was one of them."

"I didn't know," Teddy said. "Bisabuelo knew El Tigre's real name. He said El Tigre was a Cubano."

"No, he was from the Dominican Republic. Santo Domingo, they called it then," said Al Molina. "It's a shame that few Latinos know their own history. Most of the world thinks that all the great cowboys and gunfighters were guys who looked like John Wayne and Alan Ladd. Actually, there were many Latino lawmen. Outlaws, too. There were black cowboys and lawmen, but the history books—"

"*Mis*ter Molina," called a member of the TV crew, waving a microphone as though it were a magic wand. "*Can* we get this done today?" The Champion waved an acknowledgment to the crewman and then turned to Teddy.

"Look, Tiger," Al Molina said. "I have to do this TV show, and there's a shoot in a few minutes. Looks like we're holding up the parade." The Champion reached into his shirt pocket and produced a business card.

"Here's my name and number. I'd be very interested to see this pistol your bisabuelo gave to you. It may be quite valuable. Some of those old pieces are—"

"*MIS*ter Molina!" called the TV technician again.

"Gotta go," said The Champion hurriedly. "Watch the shoot, Tiger. I'll talk to you afterwards. If I get too busy, call me at my office on Monday, okay?"

"Sure thing, Mr. Molina," Teddy said.

The Champion turned to go. Halfway to the spot where the TV technician waited, he turned and called softly to Teddy, "One more thing, Tiger. Call me Al."

"You bet . . . Al!" called Teddy, grinning from ear to ear.

While The Champion was busy talking into the microphone, Teddy looked over the setup for the contest. There was a large, heavy wooden backstop. To stop the bullets, Teddy thought. In front of the backstop, about three feet in front, were two metal hoops, each about a foot in diameter. The hoops were set on heavy steel bases with iron rods, adjustable for height.

Inside each hoop was an ordinary kid's toy balloon, blown up to a diameter of four inches. On the outside diameter of each hoop, directly above the center of each balloon was a small light bulb, set behind a heavy glass lens. As Teddy watched the equipment being tested, one of the light bulbs flashed brightly, visible even in the strong sunlight of the California afternoon.

A man in western garb was adjusting the equipment and testing it further. He had the legend Compadres Gun Club embroidered across the back of his shirt. He waved to another man, seated behind the controls of some electronic device Teddy didn't recognize. The light bulb flashed again.

The man in the embroidered shirt then went to a point eight feet away from the balloons. He checked the distance with a steel tape rule, and placed a strip of masking tape on the concrete floor of the enclosed area. Satisfied with his work, the man nodded to the operator of the controls. "All set," he called.

"Ladies and gentlemen," said the park loudspeakers, "The Fast Draw exhibition is about to begin at the Roaring Twenties Pavilion!"

David Hoar, who had been listening to the playback of Al Molina's explanation of the rules, evidently felt he now knew enough to explain the proceedings to the crowd. He picked up the mike.

"Ladies and gentlemen," Hoar said, "the two targets you see before you are stationed eight feet from the firing line. Above the targets, you will see a small light . . . Will someone please flash that?" The lights above both balloons obligingly flashed. "Now, that is the signal for the shooter to fire," continued David Hoar. "Our gunslinger will attempt to shoot out both of those balloons. I might add that the targets are six feet apart, and eight feet from the shooter. At the instant that little light flashes, our own Wyatt Earp will try to shoot first one, then the other balloon, as fast as he can."

Teddy got as close to the protective railing as he could. This was something he *had* to see up close. David Hoar was still explaining.

"And to give you an idea, folks, of how it all works, here is the World's Fastest Draw. Mr. Al Molina of Los Angeles. Let's give him a really super hand!"

The Champion approached the firing line where Hoar waited, mike in hand. He stood alongside the Englishman and made a few small adjustments to his gunbelt. Then in a motion so fast that Teddy almost missed seeing, Molina drew his pistol and reholstered it. Teddy blinked. It had been so fast! Hoar, unimpressed, continued.

"Now will you tell our TV audience, Al, what you'll be doing?"

"When that light flashes, I shoot," said Al Molina simply. "The lights are connected to an electronic timer. Once the timer is set, the light will flash no sooner than two seconds, and no longer than five seconds from when the timer calls 'Shooter set!' "

"Super," said David Hoar. "Now, I'll just move back out of your way. Heh-heh-heh."

"Shooter on the line!" called the man at the timing equipment.

The Champion set himself at the line, within the taped area. He again made the practice move that had so startled Teddy earlier. This time he actually clicked the trigger of his pistol a few times. Teddy saw that when Molina drew his pistol, he moved his left hand across his body and cocked the pistol with a fanning motion. The boy's great-grandfather had told him about fanning a gun, but Teddy had never seen anyone do it.

The man in the embroidered shirt, now wearing an apronlike garment about his waist, reached into one of its pockets and took out five .45 caliber shells and fitted them into the cylinder of The Champion's pistol. He then moved back to the timer board.

"Shooter set!" cried the announcer.

Al Molina went into a light crouch. Teddy's eyes were glued to the targets, waiting for the lights to flash. Which is why when The Champion drew and fired, Teddy missed seeing it. One moment, the balloons were there; a brief, loud report, and suddenly both balloons were gone! But Teddy had heard only one shot. What had happened? As if in explanation, the timer's voice came over the P.A. "Time: 47.2!"

David Hoar came forward, mike in hand. The crowd was still applauding Molina's incredible feat.

"Thank you, thank you," said David Hoar, as though he had done the shooting. "By the bye," he said, "that time you heard mentioned by the announcer . . . forty-seven, two. That means that Al Molina shot out both of those balloons in forty-seven point two HUNDREDTHS of a second! If you're wondering how fast that really is, it's ten times faster than the average eye blink! Now, let's really hear it for Al Molina and some truly super shooting!"

Teddy felt a hand upon his shoulder. He looked up to see Lorenzo Machado standing beside him. "All right, hijito," Lorenzo said. "It's all over. Let's go."

"But Papa," Teddy protested, "it's not over at all. That was only a demonstration. The real shooting hasn't started yet!"

"When you have seen one cowboy shoot a balloon, you have seen them all," said Lorenzo Machado. "Your sisters are hungry. So are your Mama and I. We cannot pay the prices for food here. We have to go now."

"But Papa—"

"But nothing. I said we are going!"

"Yes, Papa," Teddy said, his soul in the deepest anguish. How would he explain to The Champion that he couldn't stay? Close to tears as he walked behind his father, Teddy took out Al Molina's business card. Perhaps if he showed this to his father, the boy would be allowed to stay.

For the first time, Teddy read the address on the card The Champion had given to him. It read: Al G. Molina, Jr., De Soto Insurance Agency, 675430 Century Boulevard, Inglewood, CA 91765.

Teddy felt better then. The Champion's office was in Inglewood. They *would* see each other again. Teddy would make sure of that!

Nine

Teddy's hands trembled as he took the .45 with its belt and holster from the hiding place in his father's closet. He'd waited until Lorenzo had driven Luisa and his sisters to the market for groceries. Luisa, a typical New Yorker, had never driven a car. Consequently, every errand requiring a car, and in California, that is all of them, entailed Lorenzo driving Luisa to her destination.

Teddy knew well where the pistol was hidden. He'd seen the messenger arrive with the parcel from the lawyer's office the same day as the check had come. Teddy had feared at first that Lorenzo would take the gun immediately to a gun shop as the lawyer Cepeda had advised. But happily and luckily for Teddy, the gun had been delivered on a Friday, late. Over the weekend, the family's visit to Knott's precluded Lorenzo having the pistol rendered harmless.

The boy quickly inspected the pistol, sighting down the barrel. He feared there might already be melted lead in it. But no, the .45 was still intact. Teddy resisted the impulse to strap on the gunbelt and holster before the full-length mirror in his parents' room. He knew that Lorenzo and Luisa's bedroom was off limits to any of the family's children.

Hastily, he left the bedroom and went to the kitchen. He peered out the window to make sure that his parents and sisters hadn't returned early, then he picked up the telephone and dialed the number on The Champion's business card. "De Soto Insurance Agency," said a cheery female voice.

"Mr. Molina, please," Teddy said.

"Mr. Molina junior or senior?" asked the female voice.

For a moment, Teddy drew a blank. He scanned The Champion's business card again. "Mr. Molina, junior," Teddy said. After a "One moment, please," The Champion came on the line.

"Mr. Molina, this is Teddy Machado."

"Yes, Mr. Machado. What can I do for you?" said Al Molina, in a businesslike tone.

Teddy's heart sank. The Champion had forgotten who he was! "I spoke to you yesterday, at Knott's Berry Farm . . . Al," Teddy said. "I'm the one who told you about my bisabuelo's Colt .45."

"Oh sure!" said The Champion, recognition in his voice. "How you doin' Tiger?"

"Just great, Al," Teddy replied. "I've got my bisabuelo's gun for you to take a look at. Can I come over and show it to you now?"

"Gee, not now, Tiger," said The Champion. "I got a gang of paperwork this morning. How about lunch time?"

Teddy looked at the kitchen clock and groaned inwardly. It was now only ten A.M. Lunch was two hours away and his parents were bound to return before noon! Well, then let them, Teddy thought. I can't let them destroy my Colt. "Fine with me, Al," Teddy said into the telephone.

"Should I come to your office?"

"No, you don't have to. Meet me at O'Hanlon's Hardware Store. It's at . . . ," The Champion paused. "Wait. You're new to L.A., aren't you? Just get to the corner of La Cienega and Century. You'll see the sign."

Though he hadn't the remotest idea of where the named intersection was, Teddy said quickly, "I'll see you there at noon, Al."

After The Champion had hung up, Teddy went to the cupboard below the kitchen sink, where his mother prudently saved paper sacks from the market. He lovingly placed the pistol and gunbelt inside a sack marked Alpha Beta and slipped out the back door of the little house. Just as he did so, he spied the Pontiac carrying his family coming down the street.

Teddy quickly hid in the narrow passageway between the garage and the small house. Once the Pontiac entered the driveway, he waited until he had heard the Machados go into the house. He then slipped out onto the street and down the block, toward Century Boulevard. His heart was still pounding.

Al Molina's directions had been unnecessary. Teddy found

the intersection easily. It was only a few blocks from where the Machados lived. And O'Hanlon's Hardware Store wasn't a hardware store at all. It was a gun shop, with a large, easily recognized sign in the shape of an old Colt revolver.

Teddy had wondered about that when The Champion had mentioned the name of the place, but had been too embarrassed to ask Molina for details. After all, he didn't want The Champion to think him dumb.

Despite a sign in the glass paneled door that read, "Yes, We're Open," when Teddy peered in through the glass, the shop appeared empty. He didn't want to enter a strange place, and decided to wait for The Champion to arrive. Teddy passed some time gazing into the display window.

Being a New Yorker, Teddy was totally unprepared for the assortment of items on display. In New York, it is near-impossible for the average citizen to purchase a firearm of any description. And handguns, in particular, are severely controlled. Teddy couldn't believe what he saw.

There were pistols of all calibers, .32's, .22 target pistols with long barrels and elaborate handgrips, rifles, shotguns and cleaning kits. There was even a showcase of the most ornately worked hunting knives Teddy had ever seen.

But the item that caught Teddy's eye lay in the center of the assorted instruments of sport and mayhem. Set in a red velvet framed background was an exact duplicate of the Colt .45 Teddy carried in the paper sack at his side!

He looked up and down the street and saw no sign of Al Molina. Maybe he's already inside, someplace, Teddy thought. Screwing up his courage, Teddy pushed through the door and entered the gun shop.

In response to a bell triggered by the door opening, a small, wiry man in his late thirties came out of a rear work area and up to where the cash register was. The man was fair-haired with blue-green eyes that seemed constantly in motion, as though always on the alert. He walked as though he had steel springs inside his shoes.

From the wiry man's aggressive appearance, Teddy expected him to be rough-spoken. The boy was surprised when the man said in a voice hardly louder than a whisper, "Yeah, kid. What can I do for you?"

"You're from New York!" said Teddy in surprise.

"Yeah. Howdja know?" said the man in pure Brooklynese.

"From the way you talk," Teddy said. "I'm from New York, too."

Teddy didn't comment that the man had an accent so thick, it could have supported a neon sign labeled Brooklyn.

"Yeah?" said the wiry man. "That's funny. I useta have a heavy accent when I came here, years ago. But I mostly lost it now." The wiry man smiled, displaying a set of pearly white teeth so perfect that they had to be dentures. The smile converted the man's face from its former ferretlike look into an expression of charming boyishness.

"But what can I do fer ya?" he concluded.

"I'm supposed to meet someone here," Teddy said. "Al Molina."

"Why dincha sayso?" said the small man, grinning broadly now.

"Any friend of Al's . . . ." He extended his hand to Teddy. "I'm O'Hanlon," he said. "Tom O'Hanlon. I got some coffee goin' in the back. Want some?"

"Pleased to meet you," said Teddy, taking O'Hanlon's grip. As he did, he noticed that the wiry man's hands were heavily callused across the lower edges and heavily knobbed growths punctuated his knuckles as well. The handshake was firm and O'Hanlon's palms were dry.

"I'm Teddy Machado, from New York," said the boy.

"Nice t'meetcha," said O'Hanlon. "Whatcha got in the sack?"

Teddy reached inside the paper sack and grasping the pistol grip, drew the weapon from its holster. The reaction from O'Hanlon was stunning. In one fluid motion, the little man vaulted the counter. With a single sweep of his hand, he disarmed the boy. The next thing Teddy knew, the Colt was in O'Hanlon's hand.

Teddy drew back in fear. The little man's blue-green eyes had become bright blue, and to the boy, it seemed as though tiny points of red flame burned within. It was as though O'Hanlon had become some sort of wild animal! But as quickly as it had come, the look faded from the wiry man's face. He opened the cylinder of the old Colt and satisfied himself that the weapon was unloaded.

"Jeezzuss, kid, don't do that!" whispered O'Hanlon. "Never point a pistol, full or empty, at anyone. You scared the crap outa me!"

"I'm sorry," said Teddy, thoroughly ashamed. "I didn't know."

"Well, now ya know," said O'Hanlon. Then, looking at the pistol closely for the first time, O'Hanlon exclaimed, "Hey, where'dja get this? It's beautiful. Just beautiful!"

The little man walked back behind the counter, motioning Teddy to follow him. He laid the pistol on a soft cloth spread out in the middle of a cluttered workbench. He then swung a bright lamp directly over the pistol, where it lay. He took a pair of safety shielded eyeglasses from his pocket and slipped them on.

"I don't believe this," said O'Hanlon. "Let me check out the serial number on this piece."

He reached below his workbench and withdrew a heavy, steel-bound ledger book and began leafing through its pages. He nodded to himself, as though the ledger book's information merely confirmed something he already knew. He turned to Teddy, smiled and said,

"Six hunnerd and fifty bucks. Not a penny more."

"You don't understand," said Teddy. "I don't want to sell it."

Teddy quickly explained to O'Hanlon the reason he brought the pistol to the gun shop. He told the entire story. When Teddy came to the part where Cepeda had recommended melted lead down the gun barrel, O'Hanlon swore softly.

"Greasy bastard," he whispered. "All them lawyers are so scared of guns that they crap in their pants every time they walk by a gun shop. They oughta all be—"

At this moment, the bell at the front door rang, and Al Molina came into the shop. Teddy never did find out what O'Hanlon thought should happen to all lawyers. But Teddy had the idea that it wouldn't have been pleasurable.

For a few minutes, O'Hanlon and The Champion chatted about things and people Teddy didn't know, in terms he didn't understand. Teddy knew that the two men were discussing firearms, but the language they used was so esoteric that he barely understood them.

Teddy glanced at the wall clock near the cash register. It was getting late, and Teddy was beginning to worry. He knew that somehow he would have to replace Benito Machado's Colt in its hiding place without his father being the wiser. Teddy cleared his throat. Al Molina looked at him and said:

"Sorry Tiger. We were wrapped up in something else. Say, have you two met?"

"Yeah, we met," O'Hanlon said. "Nice kid."

"His friends call him El Tigre," said Al Molina. "Did you know about that, Tee?"

"I can believe that," smiled O'Hanlon. "He took me by surprise a little while ago."

"Took *you* by surprise?" said Molina, eyebrows raised. "That's a little tough to do with a karate master."

"Just kiddin'," said O'Hanlon to Al Molina, winking at Teddy.

Teddy sighed in relief. He'd thought for a moment that O'Hanlon was going to tell The Champion about the bad mistake Teddy had made earlier. In that second, though he didn't know it, Tom O'Hanlon acquired a staunch friend and admirer in Teddy Machado.

"Say, did you see the Colt this kid's got?" O'Hanlon asked of The Champion. "I got it back on the bench."

"He told me about it, but I haven't seen it."

"I have the belt and holster, too," Teddy offered. He looked askance at O'Hanlon. "Okay to take it out of the sack?"

"Sure, kid, sure," said O'Hanlon as the three walked into the back room of the gun shop. The wiry little man went to his bench and pointed a finger at the iron bound ledger book Teddy had seen him consult earlier. "Lookit here," he said.

Teddy did as instructed. On the indicated page of the book was an illustration of a Colt pistol. It appeared identical to the Colt given Teddy by his bisabuelo.

"Now what you got here," began O'Hanlon in a lecturer's tone, "is your .45 single-action Army Colt. They used to call it The Peacemaker, too. It was made in a gang of calibers, but .45 is the commonest. Stock model was a seven and a half inch barrel, stained walnut grips, with a blued finish."

Teddy had no idea what O'Hanlon was talking about. All Teddy really knew about handguns was that they went bang when you pulled the trigger, and a bullet came out of the business end. All this talk about actions and calibers might just as well have been Chinese to the boy. But O'Hanlon went on with his lecture as though Teddy understood each unfamiliar term.

"This was a very successful model," O'Hanlon continued. "Colt made it from 1873 to 1940, with very few changes. Now, the serial number on this pistol of yours is number 6285. That means it was made in 1881. Tell me, kid, did your great-grandpa get this new?"

"No, Mr. O'Hanlon," Teddy replied. "He got it as a gift in 1916. He was almost 90 years old when he died this year."

"This piece hadda be easy 20 years old when he got it," O'Hanlon said. "But that don't mean a thing with these old babies. They made 'em good back then. Clean this one up, you could probably fire it right now."

O'Hanlon sighted down the barrel of the old pistol. "It's filthy inside, but at least it ain't rusty."

"What would you say it's worth?" asked The Champion.

"I'd give 650 for it. Clean it up and reblue it, I could get maybe eight big ones from a collector," O'Hanlon replied.

The Champion put a hand on Teddy's shoulder and said, "Well, Tiger, it seems you have a valuable piece of hardware there. Not so good as a working pistol. I know I couldn't use it for what I do. But there's no doubt that your bisabuelo's pistol is a true bit of American history, all right."

"Not for long, it won't be," said O'Hanlon.

He explained to The Champion what Lorenzo Machado and the lawyer had planned for the old weapon. As Teddy heard O'Hanlon recount the tale, he saw the expression on The Champion's face shift from wonder through outrage, then quiet anger.

When O'Hanlon had finished, Al Molina turned to Teddy and asked, "How did you get it safely here, Tiger!"

Somewhat embarrassed, Teddy told of how he stole into his parents' room and further explained that he had to replace the gun before it was missed. Either that, or face Lorenzo Machado's anger.

"Maybe you could come with me to my house and explain?" Teddy asked of Molina.

"You know better than that, Tiger," said The Champion. "I would tell anyone anywhere the value of the Colt. But the other thing; swiping it from your folks' bedroom, that's different. That's between you and your papa. You'll have to work that one out alone, Tiger."

"I'll tell him, then," said O'Hanlon. "I'll tell him good!"

"That's another thing El Tigre doesn't need," said Molina shaking his head. "O'Hanlon, you know more about guns than anyone I've ever met. But when it comes to things like this, face it. You're nobody's diplomat."

"Yeah, I guess yer right," answered the wiry little man. "But still and all, aincha gonna help the kid?"

"If I can, if I can," said The Champion.

Then to Teddy, he said, "What if I drove you home right now, Tiger? Could you put the gun back where you got it?" Teddy explained the impossibility of the task.

"Then it looks like to me that you're going to have to talk to your papa man-to-man, Tiger. Maybe if you explain to him how valuable the piece is, he'll go lighter on you. It's kind of like throwing good money away, what he wants to do with the gun."

"Hey, that might work!" said Teddy brightening. "He's always rappin' about money. Making it, saving it, spending too much of it. But . . . it's not his pistol. It's mine. So, it wouldn't be *his* money."

"I see," said Al Molina. He smiled ruefully. "Then I guess you'll just have to work it out as best you can."

"I got it!" cried O'Hanlon.

In that moment, Teddy understood why O'Hanlon rarely spoke above a whisper. When he did, his voice cracked, like an adolescent's. But Teddy couldn't imagine anyone laughing at Tom O'Hanlon's voice. Or at anything O'Hanlon did. Not after seeing him in action, anyway. O'Hanlon continued excitedly:

"Look. I'll take some of my commercial stationery and give the kid a professional appraisal, like I do for estates and stuff. And what's more, I'll say in the appraisal that if the Colt is monkeyed with, it makes it worthless. I mean, even if it ain't his own gun, his old man ain't gonna screw it up then. It'd be like settin' fire to money!"

"I can pay for the appraisal," Teddy offered. "My bisabuelo left me some coins, too."

"Did I ask you for anything?" said O'Hanlon coolly.

"Lighten up, Tee," said Al Molina. "Tiger didn't mean anything by that remark. He was trying to say thanks, that's all. Right, Tiger?"

"Sure," Teddy replied. "I didn't mean to insult you, Mr. O'Hanlon."

"Awright, awright," said the wiry little man, mollified. "I'll start out on the appraisal right now. It'll take some time, though. I'm a rotten typist. Did you wanna use the back room, Al? You won't bother me none, if you do."

"Sure do want to use it," replied Molina. "El Tigre here wants to see what Fast Draw is all about."

"Help y'self, Al. You know where the key is at . . . ."

With Teddy in tow, Al Molina got a key ring from O'Hanlon's bench and walked over to what Teddy had thought to be the back door of the gun shop. The Champion opened the door and switched on a light. Teddy now could see that the gun shop was actually much larger and deeper than it appeared.

The room was long, the length of the shop, and about 12 feet wide. At the far end was a complete target setup. Standing in a corner were exact duplicates of the Fast Draw equipment Teddy had seen at Knott's. Molina told Teddy to stay put, and left the room.

In a few minutes he returned carrying Teddy's gunbelt, holster and Colt .45 pistol. In his other hand, he held a carrying case about the size of an overnight bag. He handed Teddy the old Colt. "Strap it on, El Tigre," he said.

"Right now?" asked Teddy.

"You said you wanted to be a shooter, didn't you?"

"Errr . . . yeah."

"Then you start by strapping on your rig. I cleaned your pistol for you. Put it on while I get set up here."

Quickly, Teddy put on the gunbelt. Even with the belt buckled at the last notch, the pistol hung close to Teddy's right knee. He watched as Al Molina opened the leather carrying case.

The inside of the case was lined in purple velvet, and there were separate compartments for The Champion's belt, holster and pistol. Below that was a set of drawers containing ammunition, cleaning and repair tools. On the inside cover of the case was a brass plaque that read: "Alberto Molina, Jr., World's Champion Fast Draw." The Champion saw Teddy's interest and said:

"I didn't get it for myself, Tiger. It was a gift from my dad. It *is* a neat case, though, isn't it?"

"You mean your dad *likes* the idea that you're a . . . shooter?" asked Teddy in wonder.

"Who do you think taught me how to shoot?" said Molina, smiling.

"Now, let me get your pistol loaded up here."

Molina held out his hand to Teddy, and the boy realized that he was supposed to hand over his pistol. He drew it carefully from the holster and gave it to Molina butt end first. Teddy hadn't forgotten the earlier incident with Tom O'Hanlon.

The Champion went to his gun case and took out a handful of what to Teddy appeared to be empty bullet casings until he noticed that the ends of the casings were sealed.

"This is what you'll be shooting, El Tigre," said Al Molina.

"It's a casing that contains only a very small charge of powder. It's called a primer charge, and you can see that the shell casing is plugged with wax at the other end."

The Champion pointed to a vertical sheet of plywood, with a plexiglass window a foot square. Behind the window was an ordinary light bulb.

"When you fire, the primer charge will shoot the wax plug out, and the wax will leave a mark on that target board. And don't worry," Molina said, "you won't break the little window."

"You mean you don't shoot real bullets?" asked Teddy in wonder.

"What in the world for?" laughed The Champion. "You don't need a lead slug to leave a mark on a target. Or to break a balloon, either."

"You weren't shooting real bullets out at Knott's Berry Farm, then?"

"Never. Too dangerous with all those people around," explained Al Molina. "When you shoot at balloons, you use a heavier charge of powder, with a paper plug at the end of the casing. It's actually the unburned powder that breaks the balloons. The cardboard plug is burned up when you fire. The rest of the powder shoots out the muzzle and busts the target. But make no mistake. You can get a nasty burn from it. Just because you're not shooting real ammo in Fast Draw doesn't mean you can be careless. Never, ever, be careless with a pistol."

Al Molina noted Teddy's expression and asked, "What's the matter, Tiger? Disappointed we don't use real slugs?"

"Well, I thought that—"

"That we used lead slugs? Sorry, Teddy. But if it makes you feel any better, we could shoot real slugs, if we wanted to. Fast Draw rules require that the pistol you use *should* be able to fire real ammo. It's just that nobody in Fast Draw ever does. *That's* against the rules, in fact.

"It's cheaper than firing real ammo, but most of all it's safer. Did you know that in the entire 25-year history of Fast Draw as a sport, that no one has ever been hurt?"

"I sure didn't."

"Well, there you go, Tiger," said Al Molina. "Name me another sport, with or without special equipment, that has a safety record like that. You can't name a one. Anyway, are you ready?"

Teddy was torn. He didn't want to admit to The Champion that he had never fired a gun in his young life, except for his matched cap pistols. Somehow, Teddy didn't think that counted. He felt a sinking sensation in his stomach as he saw Al Molina fit a wax-tipped cartridge into the cylinder of Benito Machado's old Colt. And when The Champion handed the pistol to Teddy, the boy hoped that the trembling of his hand wasn't noticeable to Molina.

Being careful not to point the pistol at anything but the floor, Teddy placed it in the holster at his side. He noticed that The Champion hadn't yet strapped on his own shooting rig. He came over and stood next to Teddy, a hand on the boy's shoulder.

"Okay, Tiger," Molina said, "I want to show you how it works. I'll set the timer. Then you'll see. Once I call 'Shooter set!,' you watch that little light bulb behind the plexiglass window. In a few seconds, the bulb will light up. That's your signal to draw and fire."

The Champion's face grew stern. "Now, for God's sake, don't try to draw fast! I want you to do it all in slow motion. Ver-r-ry slow motion. This Colt of yours is not a Fast Draw weapon. Neither is your belt and holster. Fast Draw equipment is very specialized. But using your bisabuelo's Colt will at least give you some of the feel of it, okay?"

"Okay," said Teddy, trying to sound confident and in control.

"Good!" said The Champion making an adjustment on the timing machine controls. "You ready now?" he asked. Teddy nodded. "Shooter set!" called Al Molina.

At first, Teddy thought that the timer light might be blown out. It seemed as though he'd stood there at the ready for minutes. Then suddenly, the light behind the plastic window flashed!

Teddy's hand flew to his side in a motion he'd been practicing with cap pistols for three years.

"Pow!" cried Teddy, shaking the unfired Colt at the target, "Pow! Pow!"

The boy looked over at The Champion, who seemed suddenly to have taken a fit of coughing. Molina turned his back to Teddy, and The Champion's shoulders shook uncontrollably for a few seconds.

Teddy stayed where he was, the pistol still pointed at the light bulb, which had remained lighted. When The Champion finally turned around, Teddy could see the man's eyes were red, from coughing.

"Uh, Teddy . . . ." said Al Molina softly. "When you fire, pull back on the hammer as you draw and aim. Then, when the pistol is fully cocked, you squeeze the trigger."

He put a hand to his mouth, as though he were about to cough again. Once in control of himself again, The Champion added, "The gun will go *pow*. You don't have to."

Ten

"You should have told me you'd never fired a real gun before," said Al Molina to Teddy.

"I would have, Al, but I didn't think you'd show me anything if I told you," Teddy replied. His face colored slightly. "I didn't want you to think I was a turkey," he added.

The Champion pulled two chairs up to the timing equipment table. He sat down and motioned for Teddy to sit as well. "I can see that this may take some time," Al Molina said.

Then noting the disappointed look on Teddy's face, he added:

"Don't worry, Tiger. I ain't quitting on you. I just can't have you so much as handling a pistol if you don't know anything about it."

The Champion reached across the table and opened his gun case. He removed a few implements. He then had Teddy watch closely as he laid Benito Machado's Colt upon the tabletop.

"I'm going to show you just what you got here, and how it works, Teddy," The Champion explained. "I don't pretend to be a gunsmith like O'Hanlon, but I do know this particular weapon as well as any man."

The Champion laid out a gunsmith's screwdriver, a pair of parallel-jawed pliers and a few pieces of chromed steel, which he identified to Teddy as punches. As he spoke to Teddy, Al Molina began disassembling the old Colt.

"Tell me, Teddy," Molina asked, "have you ever set off a firecracker under a tin can?"

"A coupla times," Teddy admitted.

"And what happens when you do that?"

"The can flies way high up in the air."

"Right, Tiger. And the thing that makes the can fly is expanding gases from when the firecracker explodes. See, the inside of the tin can fills with those gases, and the can gets pushed straight up in the air." The Champion held up the cylinder which he had just removed from the old Colt.

"Now, when you place a cartridge into a chamber of this cylinder, and the hammer falls, setting off the charge, the chamber of this cylinder gets like the tin can. It fills with gases.

"Now, the bullet can't fly backwards at you because this piece here stops it. That's called the recoil plate." The Champion indicated the section. "So whatever is in the end of the cartridge, whether it's a bullet or a wax plug, has only one direction to go . . . out this long tube, which is called—"

"The barrel," said Teddy.

"Right on, Tiger," said The Champion smiling broadly. "That's the barrel. Now, each time you pull back on the hammer, to cock the pistol, these springs and gizmos turn this part, to put a new cartridge under the hammer. Do you know what this is called?"

"The cylinder?" Teddy asked.

"Right again!" cried Al Molina. "You're catching on just fine!"

Over the next hour, Teddy learned the proper names and the uses of all 47 parts to the old Peacemaker. When O'Hanlon entered the back room of his shop, he heard Teddy reciting as Molina pointed at each piece of the disassembled Colt laid out on the timing equipment table.

"Backstrap, backstrap screws . . . barrel . . . base-pin . . . ."

"Not bad, not bad at all," said O'Hanlon as he joined the two. "Gonna make the kid into a gunsmith, huh?"

"No Tom," Molina replied. "Just showing El Tigre what his Colt is all about."

"Too bad you ain't teachin' him, Al," said O'Hanlon. "You'd make a good teacher. Maybe even a gunsmith, if you'd pay more attention to the machinery. But you'd rather play cowboy."

"Hey, that's what my dad calls it," Teddy said. "Playing cowboy."

"In a way, that's what it is, Tiger," said Al Molina. "But the way we play the game, nobody gets hurt. It's like fencing. You don't fence with sharp points and edges on the swords. You go for the sport. But fencing is one-on-one. With Fast Draw, you're fighting the clock."

"And yourself," added O'Hanlon. "Fighting yourself is the toughest part."

"Tom doesn't believe in Fast Draw," Molina explained to Teddy. "He's a hunter. He's been a professional soldier all over the world. He thinks Fast Draw is Mickey Mouse stuff."

"Ah, don't get me started," said O'Hanlon, waving a callused hand. "You awready know how I feel about it. A handgun is a man killer. That's what you're practicing: killing. You can shoot wax or wad at targets all day. But don't kid yourself. Killing is what you're practicing."

"All right, then," countered Al Molina. "What about your black belt in karate? When you go through your *katas* and break boards and bricks, what are *you* practicing?"

"Killing . . . sometimes," said O'Hanlon grudgingly. "But not all karate blows are death blows. And I don't kid myself about what I'm doing. Besides, karate is a sport, with a whole philosophy behind it."

"And so is Fast Draw, Tiger," said Al Molina to Teddy. "So is Fast Draw. The difference between me and Tom is that I'm not so blood-thirsty. I don't think I'm capable of gunning a man down. Oh, I know how to do it, and all. I just think that if push came to shove, I couldn't shoot a living creature. Hell, I don't even go out hunting, like O'Hanlon does. It just isn't my style."

As he spoke, The Champion had reassembled Teddy's Colt, his lean graceful fingers seeming to fly. He checked the weapon once more, then opened the cylinder and inserted a single wax-tipped cartridge. He handed the pistol to Teddy, then strapped on his own belt and holster. Teddy noticed immediately that The Champion's belt and holster were considerably different from his own.

"Okay, Teddy," said Molina. "I'll show you how Fast Draw works. First, take out your pistol and aim it at the target."

Teddy obeyed, the heavy pistol wobbling somewhat in his hand as he held it at arm's length.

"Now cock the hammer," instructed The Champion. Teddy did so.

"All set," Teddy replied.

The Champion remained standing where he was, next to Teddy. Tom O'Hanlon took the controls of the timing equipment board. "Okay, Tiger," said Molina. "When that light comes on, you pull the trigger and fire. Got it?"

Teddy glanced at The Champion's rig. Molina's pistol was still holstered; his hands away from his body. "But I already got my gun out and aimed," protested Teddy.

"Don't worry about it, kid," called O'Hanlon from the timing table. "He's gonna beat you out anyway."

The wiry little man punched a button on the timer. "Ready on the line!" he called.

Al Molina went into a light crouch. He glanced over at O'Hanlon and nodded.

"Shooter set!" called O'Hanlon, punching another button on the machine.

Teddy waited for the light bulb to flash, every nerve in his body set to respond when the signal came. This time, it flashed almost at once. Teddy pulled the trigger of the old Colt . . . .

The report from Al Molina's pistol didn't spoil Teddy's aim. It came far too quickly for that. Before Teddy could finish pulling the trigger of the old Colt, The Champion had drawn, aimed, fired and reholstered his gun! Teddy looked with awe at Al Molina.

The boy realized in a rush, that he had been standing with a fully cocked pistol, already drawn and aimed. Yet The Champion, with his pistol still holstered and his hands *away from his sides*, had fired before Teddy could react to the signal!

"Not bad time," called O'Hanlon. "Forty two—"

"Time!" cried Teddy suddenly. "My gosh, what time is it? I have to get home!"

"Almost half past two," said O'Hanlon. "And you still ain't got your act together. What are you gonna tell your old man? I mean, I got your appraisal here, if it'll help." O'Hanlon held up a piece of letterhead stationery.

"That's not all his problem, Tom," said Al Molina. "You see, El Tigre wants to get into Fast Draw. Now he needs a pistol, belt and holster. And that costs money."

Molina noted the look of dismay on Teddy's face. He slowly drew his pistol from its holster and held it alongside the Colt Teddy still clutched in his hand. Teddy saw the difference between the two immediately.

"Yuh see the difference?" asked O'Hanlon. "That gun of Al's has a shorter barrel. The cylinder is made outa titanium. It's lighter than steel and just as strong. Any excess steel has been cut off the frame of the piece."

The little man took the gleaming pistol from Al Molina's outstretched hand. "The whole idea is to make the gun as light-weight as possible," O'Hanlon continued. "The only thing *added* to the pistol is this extension here, on the hammer. That's so you can fan it easier."

"Did you do all this?" asked Teddy.

"Nah," O'Hanlon said, pushing his free hand away, as though declining an offer for a second helping of dinner. "It ain't my work. Guy name of Jim Vandenberg down in Orange County does 'em. Does a helluva job, too."

Teddy admired Al Molina's modified Colt. To the boy, it was a thing of rare beauty. Not only had changes been made in it, but somehow, the pistol looked lighter and more graceful than his old Colt. The shiny plating made it look like a movie cowboy's gun.

"Could my Colt be made like that?" Teddy asked.

"Say kid, you're somethin' else," laughed O'Hanlon. "First you risk yer ass savin' the gun from yer old man, now you wanna fool with it. You wanta play cowboy, you get yerself a new gun and have it modified. And that ain't cheap to do, either."

"He's right, Tiger," said Al Molina, "Fast Draw pistol with modification would cost you easy $450. A belt and holster would be another hundred and a half. That's a lot of money."

"But I *have* money," Teddy protested. "My bisabuelo left me five hundred in his will."

"Not enough, kid," said O'Hanlon. "You're a hundred bucks light. And that ain't all the expenses. There's the ammo, the tools and the cleaning kit. You just ain't got enough bread."

"But he's pretty close to it, Tee," said Molina. He turned to Teddy and asked, "Do you have a job, Tiger?"

"Gee, no," said Teddy. "I just got out here this month. I ain't even seen the high school I'll be going to." Teddy thought for a moment. "And I never had a job before. I don't know how to do anything. Maybe I ought to give up the whole idea . . . ."

"C'mon, Teddy. That's no way to talk," chided The Champion. "Your bisabuelo wouldn't have given up, would he?"

"No . . . ."

"Then don't you be a quitter, either!" said The Champion.

"We're only talking a few hundred bucks. If you had a job, I could loan you the money. Then you could pay me back while you're learning."

"Swell," chimed in O'Hanlon. "Except that the kid don't have no job. Where's he gonna get one?"

"Oh, I don't know, Tee," said The Champion, looking around the shop. "But I *do* know this gun shop where the owner has to keep going back and forth from workbench to counter when a customer comes in . . . ." Molina winked at Teddy. "And the floor gets swept once a week, whether it needs it or not," he continued.

"Oh no yuh don't!" O'Hanlon said quickly. "I like things here just the way they are!"

"Sure you do," said The Champion. "That's why you're so far behind in your repair work. You love waiting on customers so much that you've got dust on the workbench!"

Teddy watched and heard the conversation between Molina and O'Hanlon like a spectator at a tennis match, his head moving from side to side.

"This here is a one-man operation," O'Hanlon said. "I can handle it alone."

"Nobody said you couldn't, Tom," soothed The Champion. "But just think of all you could get done if you had someone to help you."

"The kid's under age," said O'Hanlon. "He ain't allowed to wait on customers. It's the law."

"There's no law says he can't handle a broom," said Molina.

"Or clean windows and showcase glass. He could run errands, too. Get your lunch for you up the block. He could unpack stock. And you could teach him little things to help you. That way you could finish making that long rifle you promised my father two years ago. And—"

"Awright! Awright awready!" protested O'Hanlon. "I'll think about it."

"Think about this, then," said Al Molina. "El Tigre has to go home and face off his father now. Think of what a difference it would make if when he got home, he could tell his dad that the Colt is valuable."

"That's why I wrote the appraisal," O'Hanlon said.

"Okay, Tee. Now think about if Teddy could show his father the appraisal and tell him besides that he got himself a job. That'd make quite a difference, wouldn't it, Tiger?" Molina said.

"It sure would," Teddy replied. "He ain't found a job for himself yet. He went out looking last week. No luck yet, though."

"Don't you see, O'Hanlon?" asked Molina. "You can make it all right for El Tigre to go home. C'mon. Give him a chance at least."

O'Hanlon sat down at the timing table. He glanced over at Teddy. The boy was watching him as a spaniel watches mouthfuls at a dinner table.

"Oh, awright, fercrissakes," said O'Hanlon, grudgingly. "I'll give it a try."

"Wow!" cried Teddy.

"I said a try, kid," O'Hanlon said shortly. "But first time you screw up, you're out on your keester. Got it?"

"I got it, Mr. O'Hanlon," said Teddy grinning.

"And don't call me Mr. O'Hanlon," growled the little man. "When you keep sayin' Mr. O'Hanlon, I keep lookin' around to see if my father came in. My name is Tom. Or O'Hanlon. Or Tee. Get it?"

"Got it."

"Good!"

"You won't be sorry, Mr., uh . . . Tom," said Teddy. "I'll work real hard. I promise."

"Oh, I ain't worried about that," O'Hanlon said. "If I'm payin' you money, you'll earn it. But you better get on yer horse, cowboy. It's gettin' late."

"For me too," said Al Molina. "I have work to do. Customers to see. But I'll be back here on Monday. I can show you more Fast Draw then. Can you make it?"

"You couldn't keep me away with a .45!" said Teddy happily.

After arrangements as to pay and hours had been established with O'Hanlon, Teddy collected his Colt, put it back into the paper sack and walked out of the gun shop on a cloud. O'Hanlon watched the boy fairly dance up the street, then asked of Al Molina:

"Now what the hell is this all about? You railroad me inta givin' this kid a job. You don't even know him. A relative, I could understand. But this kid's a stranger."

The Champion sat down alongside O'Hanlon, a puzzled look on his face.

"You know?" he said. "I've been asking myself the same thing. I think it was when I met him, out at Knott's. Here's this kid I never saw before. From New York, a place I've never been. But dammit, O'Hanlon, when that kid looked me straight in the eye and said 'I want to be just like you' . . . I can't tell you what it meant to me."

"I can," snorted O'Hanlon. "It's an ego trip."

"No," said Molina carefully. "I thought about that. I mean, it *is* flattering to have a kid say that to you. But it's more than getting off on what a great gunslinger I am.

"I don't know . . . Maybe it's that I can be a hero to a Latino kid; be looked up to. That's ego. But when you think about it, Tee, how many heroes does a Latino kid have to look up to? Ball players, an actor here and there . . . .

"I never thought of myself like another Roberto Clemente, or a Ricardo Montalban. I was busy being Champ, that's all. It's all I ever wanted since I was 13, to be Champ. Okay, I'm the fastest man with a pistol in the whole goddam world. Where do I go now?"

"To work selling insurance," smiled O'Hanlon. "They don't pay you to play cowboy."

"*¡Precisamente!*" said Al Molina. "But to Teddy Machado, I'm more than an insurance salesman with an expensive hobby like Fast Draw. To him, I'm something great. Something extra special. I think I put the screws to you to give him a job because every kid should have a hero. Somebody to look up to. Teddy's hero was his bisabuelo. And now, the old man is dead. From what Teddy says, the old guy was *un hombre muy macho*. I'm flattered and honored that he chose me to take the old man's place."

"Like I said, ego."

"No! I'm saying that I have a chance to be a hero to *all* Latino kids! Hell, I just did a shoot on national television. I've been so busy working on my shooting that I've become an . . . almost-star. And never noticed it happening!

"Well, I got a responsibility to being the champion. I want to be someone that a Latin kid can look up to and say: 'Hey, *that's* my hero! And he ain't no freakin' *gringo*, Jim. He's a Latino, like me!' "

O'Hanlon regarded Al Molina with an expression that had no name on it. He stood up and began collecting the gunsmith tools that still lay on the timer's table. One by one, he carefully placed them in their proper receptacles in The Champion's guncase. He turned to Al Molina and after a pause said:

"The kid's right, Al. You *are* a Champion."

* * * * * *

El Tigre walked carefully up Century Boulevard, his Colt concealed in the paper sack. His eagle eyes watched passing horsemen and stagecoaches, ever alert. As he passed the corner turnoff to his street, El Tigre noticed a group of idlers near the corner saloon. A sign proclaiming that the bar was called Philly's Soul Restaurant hung directly above where the group of young men had gathered.

El Tigre would ignore them. They had no way of knowing that he was the fastest . . . well maybe the second fastest man in the West. He walked by, head high. As he passed, a hand clutched at the back of his T-shirt, arresting his progress.

"Now what's this we got here?" asked one of the idlers.

Jarred from his reverie, Teddy looked about him. The street before him was blocked by two large young men. Teddy estimated they were in their twenties. A glance over his shoulder confirmed his worst fears. While he'd been daydreaming, the group of idlers around the bar had formed a circle about him. All avenues of escape were cut off! One of the young men, obviously their leader, drawled:

"Let's see what you got in the sack, kid!"

Eleven

Teddy didn't hesitate for a second. He didn't have to be told what these young men were after. He knew the pattern well. People like these had been making his life miserable in New York for as long as he could recall. Teddy even knew the moves that would be made. He had seen The Barons in action in New York. This group was obviously part of a street gang.

The actions the group would take were predictable. Once the circle of tormentors had closed about him, one of the group would push Teddy off balance. While Teddy was off balance, another gang member would grab the precious parcel under his arm. Teddy had lost many sacks of groceries in just this way, while running errands for his mother in Manhattan.

It was for this reason that the members of The Flaming Avengers, Inglewood branch, had seriously misjudged their prey. Teddy had grown up on Manhattan's Upper West Side. Tough as The Flaming Avengers might appear to be, they were amateurs next to The Barons of 81st Street.

For one thing, Teddy noted immediately, they were sloppy. When they'd closed the ring around him, The Flaming Avengers had left an escape route for Teddy. The members of the circle weren't standing close enough to seal Teddy off. There was a space between one of them and the curbstone. When the shove from behind came, as Teddy knew it would, he offered no resistance. Instead, he went sharply forward, as though he were falling. He then checked his motion sharply, dropping to his hands and knees. The gang member who had shoved him then tumbled over Teddy's back and fell heavily to the pavement.

As the other members of the circle closed in, Teddy cut to his right. He darted between the outstretched, grasping hands and into the gutter. He was off and running down the street before any of The Flaming Avengers realized they'd been out-thought by a streetwise kid.

Teddy ran until an ache in his side forced him to pull up a few yards from his home. He noted with dismay that the Pontiac was still in the driveway. Lorenzo was at home. Trying to control his breathing and pounding heart, Teddy squared his shoulders and walked up the path, ready to face Lorenzo Machado's anger.

"This is the last of it!" said Lorenzo Machado later, at the dinner table. "I have put up with many things with that boy. I have been made the laughing stock of my neighborhood on two separate coasts. But this . . . tontería must end somewhere. And this is where it ends!"

Luisa Machado sat opposite her husband at the table. Alicia and Iris were washing and drying the dinner dishes. Teddy was in his room, nervously awaiting the punitive visit from Lorenzo which he knew was inevitable.

In true Latino fashion, when Lorenzo had heard of Teddy's misdeeds, he did not explode in a fit of sudden anger. That behavior was reserved for minor infringements. This was a serious matter. Teddy had stolen something from his parents' room. That what he had taken was his own property mattered not.

This deed of Teddy's called for no simple punishment. It called for a special session, behind closed doors, featuring rigorous application of the heavy leather belt around Lorenzo's waist. But first there had to be isolation, with no dinner. The idea behind this practice was that the silent solitude would afford Teddy the opportunity to contemplate his sins before the first blow of the strap fell.

Had anyone asked Lorenzo why this elaborate ritual was necessary, the asker would have been given no satisfactory reply, save, "That's the way these things are done." It had been so with Lorenzo's father, and it would be so with Lorenzo and Teddy.

Lorenzo had finished his dinner. It was now time for Teddy's punishment. Everyone in the household knew it was time. Trying to postpone the inevitable, Luisa asked of her husband: "More coffee, querido?"

"Don't try to sweet talk me, woman," said Lorenzo darkly. "The boy will have his whipping."

"Sweet talk?" asked Luisa, raising her eyebrows. "Is it sweet talk to offer my husband another cup of coffee after dinner? I thought only of your comfort and pleasure, my husband."

"You know damned well what I mean," countered Lorenzo. "It starts with sweety-sweety talk and coffee. Then, before I know what's happening, the boy doesn't get his whipping. There comes a time when talking isn't enough. He has done a serious thing, Luisa. He has stolen—"

"But the pistol is his, querido."

"As I was saying," Lorenzo continued, ignoring Luisa's remark. "He has stolen. He has disobeyed my orders and he has lied. For this, he must be punished."

"But 'Renzo, he does own the gun! Your abuelo gave it to him. And doesn't he have that piece of paper from the hardware store? It says that this pistol is worth a great deal of money. Don't you see that if you had followed Cepeda's advice, you would have destroyed a valuable piece of—"

"Crap!" snorted Lorenzo. "All guns are crap. What does a decent man want with a gun, anyway? And what difference if it's new or an antique? A gun is a gun!" Lorenzo wiped his face with his hand.

"You have talked me out of punishing the boy when he cut school. You have talked me out of whipping him when he spent his lunch monies on stupid cowboy movies. But by God, this time—"

"And he has a job now," Luisa pressed on. "'Renzo, he has never had a job in his life! Perhaps he is coming out of the dream world he lives in. You, yourself, always said—"

"I know what I've always said!" snapped Lorenzo. "Am I a senile old man, that I must be reminded of my own sayings? Don't I know what I say?"

"Ah, but this is different, querido," Luisa persisted. "He didn't try to deceive you. He didn't try to put the gun back secretly. He was truthful and . . . manly about what he had done."

"True. . . ," Lorenzo admitted grudgingly.

"And he asked for no special treatment," Luisa said. "He is fully prepared to take his whipping. He made no excuse for what he did." Luisa put a hand on Lorenzo's forearm. "In a strange way, Lorenzo, I was proud of Teddy. The way he stood up like a man and spoke his piece."

"Now you go too far!" cried Lorenzo. "The boy disobeys, lies and steals. You want me to give him a medal for it?"

"No, querido," answered Luisa. "He deserves no medal. But does he deserve a bad beating, when he was truthful and repentant about what he did?"

"But he's not repentant! He actually wants to take the money my abuelo left him and buy *another* gun! God save us all!"

"That's his choice, Lorenzo. The money is his, to spend as he sees fit. That's what abuelo's will says."

"He's too immature to make a choice," said Lorenzo.

"And if you never let him make a choice, what then?" Luisa asked. "How will he ever grow up to be the macho you want for a son? Though for the life of me, I don't see why he should be *un macho*. Is there no room in this world for gentle people? For dreamers?"

Lorenzo laughed a short, mirthless laugh. "Well, your gentle son . . . the dreamer wants to buy a gun!" he said. "Do you want to see someday in the newspaper that he has gently killed someone with a gun? Is that what you want?"

"Teddy explained all that," Luisa said. "They don't shoot real bullets in this quick draw sport."

"Aha!" exclaimed Lorenzo, like a trial lawyer fastening on a fine point of law. "He has also explained that this gun and abuelo's too, *can* fire real bullets!"

Lorenzo shook his head vehemently. "No, no matter what you say to me woman, this will not be. I will not have it!" Lorenzo Machado stood up and began to unloosen the belt at his waist. He walked down the hall to the room where Teddy waited. . . .

* * * * * *

El Tigre didn't flinch as the bullwhip fell across his back again and again. Ike Clanton was in full swing. El Tigre's catlike ears heard the hiss of the whip as it descended; felt the sear of pain as it landed. He steeled himself. He would not cry out! Many things may be said of El Tigre, he thought. But never that he cried out, or flinched from the blows of the whip.

* * * * * *

Hours later, in the darkness of their bedroom, Luisa lay sleeping while Lorenzo Machado stared at the empty blackness. "Muñeca, are you asleep?" asked Lorenzo softly.

"Not now, I'm not," answered Luisa, waking at her husband's voice. "What's the matter, honey, are you sick?"

"No, I'm fine," Lorenzo answered. "But I was thinking about Teddy. Do you know that the boy never let out a whimper? I hit him good, too. You know the way he is, Luisa. You know how he always used to try to talk me out of it? How he used to holler like an animal before the first whack?"

"I know. . . ." said Luisa sadly. "I know."

"Well, he didn't do that this time," Lorenzo went on. "He didn't say a word. When I came into his room, he just laid down across the bed. Waiting. And when I spanked him, he did not cry. Not one tear!"

"Yes, I know," Luisa said. "I heard no crying. But I heard a great deal of you, swearing. It seemed to make you angrier that he didn't cry out."

"No, that wasn't what got me so mad," Lorenzo explained. "That damn kid! I beat him good and when I was done, he just got up and looked at me, and—"

"And what?"

"He said to me, 'It doesn't matter, Papa. I won't change my mind. I will do what I will do.' Just like that. He stood there and he defied me after I had just given him the worst whipping of his life!"

"You cannot have it both ways, querido," said Luisa. "Do you want him to be a man, or a crying baby? If *the man* is what you desire him to be, that is how he reacted."

"Ahhh," groaned Lorenzo. "That boy! He won't listen, even when he is punished. He is a stubborn, muleheaded, stiffnecked—"

"Proud man," finished Luisa. "Just like his father."

"What is that supposed to mean?"

"Well, querido," said Luisa, "If I know my husband, and we have been married these 24 years, you were about to make a comment on the boy's stubbornness. Then after that you would say: 'I don't know where he gets this from!' I thought I would save you some time, querido. He gets those traits from you. No one else."

Lorenzo fell silent. Luisa was right. And in a strange way, at the moment of Teddy's defiance, Lorenzo too was proud of the boy. Teddy had taken his whipping and put Lorenzo on notice that he would not change his loco ways. In that instant, Lorenzo lost all heart for punishing the boy further. The defiance had angered him, true. But it was a cool anger Lorenzo felt. Luisa nudged him in the ribs.

"'Renzo? Are you asleep?"

"This is my final word on the subject," Lorenzo said, ignoring the question. "If the boy goes to school and gets passing grades, and he keeps this job, he may play cowboy all he wants."

"Oh, 'Renzo!" cried Luisa, cuddling close.

"Hear me out, woman," said Lorenzo sternly. "I say that he may play cowboys. But I am no longer the boy's father."

"¡Ay Diós!" exclaimed Luisa, frightened by the gravity of Lorenzo's remarks. "You cannot mean it!"

"Believe me woman, I mean it," said Lorenzo grimly. "He is no longer my son. He may live under my roof. He may eat the food I provide. I will clothe him if he is in need. If he falls ill, I will pay a doctor to heal him. But from this day, I am not his father. I will not speak to him, nor will I see his face at meals. It would spoil my appetite. I don't want to see him. And if I see him in that stupid cowboy outfit again, I'll kick his ass. Do you hear me?"

"I hear you *señor*," said Luisa. "And how long is this to go on?"

"As long as he defies me!" snapped Lorenzo. He turned over on his side and pretended he was falling asleep. He heard Luisa begin to cry softly. He felt the gentle vibrations of her sobs. He hardened his heart and continued to feign sleep.

Inwardly, Lorenzo felt a twinge of regret for the utter finality of his decision. But now it was too late. He had spoken as husband, father and head of his household. He could no longer turn back and reverse his decision. It was now a matter of amor propio; personal pride. Lorenzo had his pride. And no son named Teodoro.

Twelve

"There are 47 parts to a Colt .45 SA," recited Teddy. "The backstrap, the backstrap screws, barrel, base pin. . . ." As he recited, Teddy was assembling Benito Machado's Colt for the twentieth time in six weeks.

Tom O'Hanlon stood over the boy's shoulder as Teddy sat at the workbench in the gun shop. He watched Teddy's fingers, now nimble from practice, fly over each part as he named it. When Teddy had named and fitted into place every part of the antique pistol, O'Hanlon smiled.

"Good work, kid," he commended. "Lookin' at you doin' that, I wouldna thought you was the same kid that scared the hell outa me a few months back. You're gettin to know yer stuff."

"Gee thanks, Tee," said Teddy. "I wish I was doing this good in school."

"Ahhh, school's a lotta crap!" said O'Hanlon. "Lookit me. I got through high school by the skin of my teeth. And I'm doin' awright. I own my own business. Hell, I even own this building! Nah, I ain't done bad at all."

"I know, Tee," Teddy replied. "But that's you. Besides, my dad says that if I don't keep up my grades in school that I can't work here anymore."

"I know, kid. I know. Is he still not talkin' to you, either?"

"No, Tee. We don't even eat meals together."

"I was wonderin' why you always leave so late," O'Hanlon said. "Doncha eat dinner at all, kid?"

"Oh sure, Tee," Teddy said. "My mom saves me a plate. And when I get home, I eat dinner in my room."

Teddy saw the dark expression on O'Hanlon's face. "I don't mind, really," Teddy said hastily. "It all works out fine. I stay late here, and get a chance to practice my Fast Draw. If I went straight home, I wouldn't have a chance to practice."

"Have it your own way, kid," said O'Hanlon shrugging. "But I still say your old man's one cold bastard."

"He is not!" exclaimed Teddy heatedly. "He got his pride; I got mine. That's the way it is. But he ain't cold. He just don't understand where I'm comin' from, is all. You don't understand. You aren't a Latino. . . ."

"Ohh," said O'Hanlon elaborately. "*¿Entonces, digame. Precísamente lo que es que no entiendo?*"

"Oh, I know you speak Spanish, Tee," said Teddy. "And I know you were a professional soldier in Central America for a lot of years. But it still don't make you a Latino."

"Since when is being a Latino like joining some damn country club?" asked O'Hanlon indignantly. "Do I get in your face on account you ain't Irish?" The wiry little man's anger vanished. He smiled and asked Teddy:

"But tell me, how's yer Fast Draw?"

"Real good," Teddy replied. "Al says I'm really coming along."

"If you ain't, it ain't Al's fault," O'Hanlon observed. "Or yours either. You shoot away yer whole paycheck each week, practicin'."

"Not all of it," Teddy protested. "I got a present for my mom for her birthday. And there's still twenty bucks I owe Al Molina."

"That ain't what I mean," said O'Hanlon. "Practice, practice, practice. Doncha go to a movie once in a while. Or go out on a date, mebbe?"

"I'm not much good with the girls, Tee," Teddy confessed. "I never know what to say. And girls never want to see western flicks. And they're never interested in shooting. What can I talk about to a girl?"

"I can see this'll take some time," said O'Hanlon grinning. Lookit, kid, it's real easy with dames. When yer out with one, you talk to a dame about what interests *her* most. Her! All you gotta do is get a dame talkin' about herself, then you sit back and listen."

"I don't know. . . ," Teddy began.

"That's why I'm tellin' you," O'Hanlon said. "Now, once the dame is talkin' about herself, you don't even have to listen tight. Just listen to the tone of her voice. When she ends a sentence and her tone of voice goes down, you say 'Oh yeah.' Like sayin' ain't that a shame. If the sentence ends with her tone of voice goin' up, you say 'Oh yeah?' like she just told you somethin' you didn't know."

"And that's all there is to it?" asked Teddy doubtfully.

"That's it. I got it down to a science."

"But Tee," Teddy protested. "You've never been married. And I never heard you talk about any steady thing you got going with a girl."

O'Hanlon feigned astonishment. "Who said anything about gettin' married?" O'Hanlon cried. "I may be a gun nut, but I ain't no idiot. Lissen to me, kid. If you get married, it's like droppin' anchor. I gotta know that I can pack up my tool kit and go anywhere I want, anytime I want. I gotta be free!"

"Sure, Tee, sure. But tell me, how long have you had this shop?"

"Sixteen years," admitted O'Hanlon. "But that don't mean nothin'. I mean, I *coulda* wanted to go somewhere. I just didn't that's all. And if I was married with kids and all, I couldna gone nowhere. Do yuh see the difference?"

"Guess so," said Teddy, not seeing the difference at all.

"Well, that's neither here nor there," said O'Hanlon brightening.

"C'mon kid. Let's see yuh do some shootin'. I awready closed down the front of the shop. I'll run the timer fer yuh." He walked to the back room, where the targets were set up. Teddy followed.

* * * * * *

El Tigre knew that the moment of truth had come. He couldn't count on Wyatt, Bat and Doc this time. Maybe they hadn't received his telegram.

"I'm a-callin you out, marshal!" cried Ike Clanton from the street. "Or are yuh goin to hide in The Long Branch all day, you yella dog?"

With icy calm, El Tigre pushed aside the swinging doors of the saloon. He noted where Ike Clanton stood, in the middle of the dusty main street of Dodge City. Clanton was · ready. El Tigre was ready; he was always ready.

As El Tigre was about to step into the street, a glint of sunlight on metal caught his eye from a nearby roof. Clanton was talking tough for a reason. He had stationed a man on the roof with a rifle. El Tigre made a mental note of where he'd seen the flash of light.

A hush fell over the town as El Tigre stepped off the

board sidewalk of The Long Branch porch and into the dusty street. "Closed" and "Out to Lunch" signs sprang up like mushrooms in store windows on the main street. Merchants and customers alike retreated to the backs of the stores, out of the way of flying lead. All except for one business. Smiley, the undertaker, lounged in the doorway of his funeral parlor, a toothpick dangling from his lower lip.

"All right, Clanton," called El Tigre from 20 feet away. "Any time you're ready!"

"Come and get it!" cried Ike Clanton, making his move.

Those spectators who witnessed the historic faceoff that day still disagree. Some said that El Tigre first outdrew Ike Clanton, then got the sniper on the roof. Others say it was the other way 'round. The shots from El Tigre's pistol came so fast that no one could distinguish two separate reports.

It was as though one moment Clanton had reached for his gun, and the next he was standing there with an expression of utter disbelief on his face as the red stain spread across his shirtfront. Across the street, a form tumbled from the rooftop, bounced off the porch below and onto the street, where it lay still. The sniper's rifle, still unfired, slipped from lifeless fingers into the street. . . .

* * * * * *

"Bad time, kid," said O'Hanlon. "You ain't concentratin' hard enough. It's like you're daydreamin' out there. You gotta work yer move so you don't have to think about it. It gets almost automatic after a while. You *feel* when the light's gonna flash. Let's try it again."

Teddy worked the ejector rod on his new Fast Draw pistol and set the spent shells down on the table for reloading later. He put five new shells into the cylinder and prepared to fire the fiftieth round of the practice session. Again, he got set. When the timer flashed, he drew and fired in respectable time.

"Okay, kid. Let's knock it off fer the night," O'Hanlon said.

"I'm hungerous! Want to have a burger with me at Sally's? I'm buyin'."

Over a superburger at Sally's Restaurant nearby, O'Hanlon discussed Teddy's poor showing at the evening's practice shoot. "I think it's yer concentration, kid," he said. "You was shootin' far better time last month, when your move wasn't fast as it is now. What's buggin' yuh, Teddy?"

"I dunno," Teddy replied. "Maybe this thing with my father

is getting to me. You know we haven't said a word to each other in six weeks now?''

"So you told me, Teddy. But you also told me I don't understand it, not bein' a Latino. So I won't mix in that. But no matter what's causin' the lack of concentration, I could have the answer fer yuh. Didja ever think of takin' up karate?''

"What's karate got to do with shooting, Tee?''

"Everything, kid. Everything. See, once you get into karate you look at things different. The whole body is fine honed, like a razor. Vision, concentration, reaction time. You get fast at anything yuh wanna be fast at. . . .''

"I know," Teddy put in. "I've seen you move. Remember?''

"That's what I mean, kid," O'Hanlon persisted. "After 12 years of karate, I don't think about my moves. I see the situation and I . . . just do it, that's all.''

"But I don't have 12 years to put into it," protested Teddy.

"I don't even have 12 weeks," he continued. "There's a Fast Draw contest coming up in 10 weeks. Al says I could be ready for it, by then.''

O'Hanlon looked at the boy with fondness. Over the weeks they had spent together at the gun shop, O'Hanlon had come to like Teddy immensely. It had to do with Teddy's love for machinery; the way one thing fit into another and once properly fitted, performed flawlessly, as fine machinery should.

There had been little love in the life of Thomas Joseph O'Hanlon. Orphaned at 12 in a tenement fire in Brooklyn, he had been shuttled from relative to relative until he'd attained the age of 18. On that day, O'Hanlon went out and enlisted in the United States Marine Corps. It was timed perfectly. The month O'Hanlon enlisted, the Korean War broke out.

Five years, a Purple Heart with two Oakleaf Clusters and a Distinguished Service Medal later, O'Hanlon found himself with an honorable discharge in his hand, a Chinese machine gun bullet still lodged below his left knee, and no place to go. The small disability pension he received from the Corps was no consolation. All T. J. O'Hanlon had ever wanted to be was a fighting Marine. He was a soldier with no war to fight.

He promptly offered his services to a recruiter for a Central American government army. He was commissioned a captain, and for the next five years, until the strongman in whose army he fought was toppled from the presidential throne, he served with ferocious distinction.

At age 28, a major in a nonexistent army, O'Hanlon drew from his 10 years' experience with firearms of all descriptions. He opened his gun shop. The thousands of dollars he had earned in Central America were safely invested, for O'Hanlon's needs had always been monastic.

Once his gunsmith business was firmly established, O'Hanlon again felt aimless. It was then he was introduced to Tchai Kwo, 70 years of age and undisputed karate champion of the world. After seeing one exhibition of a frail old man tossing burly students about like stuffed dolls, O'Hanlon set out to master the most difficult of martial arts, karate.

Once established in the philosophy and discipline of karate, the wiry little man found his milieu. The fury that had raged within him since his loveless childhood found its outlet, and the philosophy taught him to control the demons in his soul. At 44 years of age, and looking 10 years younger, O'Hanlon was second only to Tchai Kwo in martial arts.

Considering his past, and having no yardstick with which to compare degrees of happiness, O'Hanlon was a fulfilled and happy man. There was an emptiness, as there had always been. But this was something with which O'Hanlon had lived since age 12.

Had O'Hanlon any experience with life other than defending or extinguishing it, he might have admitted to loneliness. But in the company of this strange Puerto Rican boy, O'Hanlon was experiencing an emotion he could not understand. He felt parental . . . protective of this boy. More than that, the boy shared O'Hanlon's one continuing interest: fine machinery, doing what it should do.

O'Hanlon snapped out of his reverie. Teddy had just said something to him. Lost in the past, O'Hanlon hadn't heard. "Sorry, kid," he said. "I was a million miles away. What didja say?"

"I said that I can't spend years learning karate," Teddy repeated. "I really want to be in the contest in December. And Al thinks I can do it, too."

"Awright," O'Hanlon said. "Tell ya what I'll do. I'm gonna teach you some karate exercises. Nah, don't look at me that way. These here exercises won't screw up yer hands like mine."

Though no illustration was necessary, O'Hanlon held his knobbed-knuckled right hand under Teddy's nose. "These exercises is for breathin' right, and gettin' yer reaction time and concentration together. C'mon back to the store with me. I'll show yuh what I mean."

"And it'll really make me faster?" Teddy asked.

"I guarantee it," O'Hanlon said.

"I'm with you then, Tee," said Teddy, following O'Hanlon to the restaurant door.

So it was that Teddy began a further course of study, and came to occupy a unique position in history. Under Tom O'Hanlon's guidance, and unknown to even Al Molina, Teddy Machado embarked upon becoming the first Zen Fast Draw in California.

Thirteen

Three weeks afterwards, arriving home from the shop later than usual, Teddy found the front door to his home locked. He noticed that the family car wasn't in the driveway. But there were lights on inside the house and he could hear music playing. Unable to open the front door, Teddy rang the doorbell. He was taken aback when the door was opened by the prettiest girl he had ever seen.

She was a few inches shorter than Teddy, but still tall enough to look him straight in the eye. Her eyes were dark and their depth had no bottom. Her glossy black hair was straight and fell well below her shoulders. The night was warm for October and she wore a low cut blouse of Indian design and a bright print skirt. She smiled at Teddy showing a near-perfect set of teeth, save for a small chip on an upper incisor. The vision of beauty spoke:

"Hi! You're Iris' brother, Teddy, huh?"

Teddy was rooted. He swallowed hard and tried to speak. But all he could manage was a nod and a mumbled, "Yeah."

"Iris is in the john," the girl said. "Come in. Your folks went to a movie. Me and Iris are babysitting for Alicia."

In a daze, Teddy followed the beautiful girl into the living room, where both the TV and FM radio were playing at maximum volume. It mattered not at all to Teddy, who heard nothing but this girl's voice. He saw nothing but her face and form. She sat down on the couch. Teddy remained standing in the middle of the room, gawking at her.

"I'm Linda Perez," said the lovely girl. "Me and Iris go to school together." What Teddy would have replied, were he capable of speech, will never be known. At this moment, his sister Iris entered the room.

"Hiya, Marshal Dillon," Iris said breezily. "Mama and Papa are at the movies. Alicia's asleep already. Why don't you sit down and be company? This is Linda Perez. We go to school together."

"Yeah, I know," Teddy said, sitting down in Lorenzo Machado's chair, opposite the TV. "Say, can we turn one of those things down a little?" Teddy asked. "Or are you watching TV and listening to the radio at the same time?"

" Gee, you sure sound like Papa," Iris said.

"Thanks a lot," said Teddy sarcastically.

Linda Perez got up from the couch and turned off both the FM and the television set. When she returned to the couch, she sat at the end nearest Teddy's chair. It was where Luisa Machado always sat when Lorenzo occupied the chair Teddy was now sitting in.

"Iris tells me that you work in a gun shop, and that you're a cowboy," Linda said.

"Iris is as funny as a split lip," Teddy said, glaring at his sister. "Yeah, I work in a gun shop. But what I am is a Fast Draw shooter. It's not being a cowboy. It's a sport. It's just like fencing is a sport. . . ." And here, thinking of the grueling practice he had just completed under O'Hanlon's tutelage, Teddy added, "Just like karate is a sport."

"Wow! That sounds neat!" Linda said. "Can I come and watch you sometime, when you practice shooting?"

"Not where I practice," Teddy said, thinking of O'Hanlon's lecture on women. "It's too dangerous," he lied.

"Ooh," said Linda Perez, her eyes growing large . . . .

* * * * * *

El Tigre helped the new schoolmarm down from the stagecoach. He turned to get her luggage from the driver. Miss Perez ascended the steps to the wooden sidewalk and walked toward The Palace Hotel entrance. She would be staying at The Palace until the little house built for her behind the school was completed. El Tigre was so busy with her luggage that he didn't notice the two idlers who blocked her path on the narrow sidewalk.

"Hey, lookit the new school teacher," one of them said, taunting.

"Say, teacher, you gonna teach me what I want to learn?" He laughed and reached out for the frightened Miss Perez.

El Tigre's kick caught the loafer square in the seat of his pants. The man whirled around, his hand already reaching for the gun at his hip. Then the idler saw to his horror, that he had almost drawn on El Tigre, himself! His face reflected the terror that was causing beads of sweat to pop out all over his brow. His hand froze, inches away from the grip of his pistol. The loafer was afraid to move a hair.

"Gee, I'm sorry, marshal," the loafer whined. "I didn't mean nothin' by it, honest. Just havin' a little fun. . . ."

"Yeah, fun. That's all," echoed the other idler. "We didn't know that she was your gal, marshal."

"You know it now," lipped El Tigre thinly. The two idlers parted like the waters of the Red Sea before Moses. El Tigre extended his left arm, and Miss Perez rested her hand lightly upon it. The two walked to the entrance of The Palace Hotel.

"Oh thank you so much, marshal," said Miss Perez, her eyes shining in open admiration. . . .

* * * * * *

"Teddy. Teddy!" cried Iris Machado. "What's the matter with you? Linda just asked you a question!"

"Sorry," Teddy said. "I was just thinking. There's going to be a Fast Draw exhibition match in December. It's in Riverside, at Frontier World. Maybe Linda would . . . er, ..."

"I'd love to go!" said Linda Perez. "I've heard about Frontier World. They say it's like seeing a western movie come alive!"

"You like western movies?" Teddy gulped, disbelieving.

"Love them," said the beautiful girl. "My favorites are the Clint Eastwoods. But I once saw one about a gunfighter, and I really dug it. It had Alan Ladd in it, and he was—"

"*Shane*," Teddy said. "Alan Ladd, Jean Arthur, Van Heflin and Jack Palance. Brandon DeWilde was the kid, Joey. Or maybe you mean *Whispering Smith*? That's the one where Alan Ladd was a railroad detective."

"No, it was *Shane*, all right. I remember now. The little boy kept calling after him, when he rode away at the end. It was sad . . . Hey, you know *all* the western movies, don't you?"

"A lot of 'em," Teddy admitted. An awkward silence fell over the room. Teddy had run out of conversation. Linda Perez was sitting right in front of him, waiting. Dammit! he thought, I can't think of a thing to say! Clumsily, he got to his feet.

"Well, I got a history exam tomorrow," he said. "Gotta study after work, you know. Can't get bounced out of school, can I? Nice meetin' you . . . uh. . . ."

"Linda."

"Nice meeting you, Linda."

Dammit again! I know the girl's name, Teddy thought furiously, why can't I seem to say it? Aloud he said:

"Uh . . . I'll tell Iris when the exhibition'll be in Riverside."

"Great!" said Linda Perez. "I see Iris every day at school. She can let me know. But maybe I'll see you before then," she added with a smile that made Teddy dizzy. "Me and Iris are real good friends . . . Teddy."

"Okay, then," Teddy concluded lamely. "See yuh."

"You will," smiled Linda Perez, confidently.

Back in his room, Teddy stared unseeing at the pages of his history textbook. For once, his mind wasn't miles away in Dodge City. His thoughts were concentrated on a place thirty-two feet, six inches from where he sat. In the living room, watching TV and again playing the FM radio, sat the object of all his thoughts.

Later that night, as he lay in bed, the house silent, save for the measured breathing of his sleeping family, Teddy said aloud to the unseen ceiling: "And she really liked *Shane*! Now what the hell do you think of that?"

Some weeks later, on a cool November evening, Luisa Machado was surprised to hear the doorbell ring. The Machados were still newcomers to their neighborhood and most of their callers were friends of the children. Luisa glanced at the kitchen clock. It was 9:30, too late for any of Iris' or Alicia's friends to be calling. With the exception of Linda Perez, whom Teddy had been seeing of late, Luisa knew her son to be a loner. Who could it be at this hour?

Years of Manhattan living had made Luisa cautious about answering the door after dark. Before she opened the door, she looked out the living room window, onto the tiny porch. She gave a sudden cry. Lying on the porch, unmoving was Teddy!

"¡Madre de Diós!" she called.

"Lorenzo, come quick! Something's happened to Teddy!"

Lorenzo dropped his newspaper and sprang from his chair in the living room. He arrived at the porch a few steps behind Luisa. She was already bent over Teddy's still form, lifting the boy's head.

In the light of the low-watt bulb on the porch, Lorenzo could see that his son's face was a mass of bruises. Further, Teddy was bleeding from a deep cut that began at his right eye and ran half way down his cheek. The boy seemed only semi-conscious.

Tenderly, Machado lifted the boy from the porch and grunted in surprise at how much weight Teddy had gained of late. In the midst of his concern, Lorenzo had the passing thought that his son was growing into a man.

Once inside the house and in stronger light, Lorenzo ignored the little cries of concern Luisa emitted as she discovered the full extent of Teddy's injuries. Quite aware of the effort it took, Lorenzo set Teddy down softly on his bed.

Luisa flew to the bathroom medicine cabinet and returned with a clean washcloth, antiseptic, bandages and tape. As she entered Teddy's room, Lorenzo was sitting on the edge of the bed talking to the boy, who was regaining his awareness.

"Who did this to you, hijito?" demanded Lorenzo. "Who did this terrible thing?"

"My hat. . . ." Teddy mumbled. "My clothes. . . ."

For the first time, Lorenzo realized that Teddy was wearing his ill-fitting western outfit. Or the remains of it. Teddy's hat, his beloved Stetson was gone. His black frontier shirt and whipcord trousers were covered with dirt and torn in several places.

"To hell with the stupid suit!" said Lorenzo. "Just tell me who did this to you!"

"A gang," Teddy said painfully through bruised lips. "The Avengers . . . they hang at Philly's Soul, on Century. . . ."

Lorenzo got to his feet, his face a mask of rage. Luisa, reading correctly Machado's intent, quickly ran to block the doorway of Teddy's bedroom.

"No, no querido!" she pleaded. "Don't be foolish! They are a gang. You heard Teddy. There are many of them!"

"Punks! ¡Mierda de perros!" snorted Lorenzo. "They are brave, beating up children. We'll see how they treat with a grown man!"

"Please, Papa, no," said Teddy weakly from the bed. "They have knives . . and a gun. . . ."

A look of realization broke over Lorenzo's features. Suddenly, his wrath was no longer directed at The Avengers. "I knew it!" he shouted, slamming his fist into his palm. "That damned gun business again! This fool here walks around looking like a freak. They stole his precious gun. That's what this is all about! The boy might just as well have worn a sign saying 'take me!'"

"No, Papa, it wasn't that way," Teddy protested. "Both my guns are at the shop."

"Then why did they do this to you?" demanded Lorenzo.

"He's hurt, Lorenzo," said Luisa dabbing at the cut below Teddy's eye. "For God's sake, let him be! Are you concerned for your son, or your damned pride?"

Machado stepped back, surprised at the vehemence of his wife's attack upon him.

"What is the matter with you, Lorenzo Machado?" continued Luisa. "Are you so wrapped up in being right that you don't care if your son loses an eye? Or gets killed in the street? Now you say it's Teddy's fault he was hurt. I don't know who's the bigger child, you or Teddy!"

Machado stood in silence, his face stony. Without another word, he turned on his heel and strode angrily into the living room. He threw himself into his chair and with whitened knuckles, gripped the newspaper he held before unseeing eyes. Luisa Machado remained in Teddy's room, ministering to her son.

Blood, bruises and cuts did not faze Luisa Machado. As the mother of two older boys, she had treated more than her share of the thumps, bumps and scrapes which small boys inevitably collect. Nor had she panicked when Jack, her eldest, had been badly slashed at a dance in New York. She regarded such happenings as a nasty, but unavoidable aspect of living in the barrio.

As she cleaned Teddy's wounds, she was relieved to see that although the injuries looked terrible, the damage done to her son was largely superficial. The cut under his eye was nowhere as deep as she first supposed. Already, the blood was clotting.

If Lorenzo had expected company from Luisa when she finished administering first aid to Teddy, he was to be disappointed. When she left Teddy's room, Luisa went directly to the girls' room. Alicia was asleep, and Iris was waiting to find out what had befallen her brother. Iris had learned from past experiences with her brother Rudi, that when such injuries took place, it was best to remain clear of all parties until the excitement died down. After tending to the girls, Luisa went directly to bed. When Machado finally came to bed, some hours later, she feigned sleep.

Teddy missed two days of school and work. On the second day, both Al Molina and Tom O'Hanlon came to visit him. Teddy, well on the mend, was immensely flattered that The Champion came to see him.

Molina explained that he could only stay a short time. Though his office was in Inglewood, the bulk of his customers were on the other side of Los Angeles, in East L.A. Molina came to Inglewood once a week, to do his paperwork. O'Hanlon remained for over two hours, talking with Teddy. It was for this reason that O'Hanlon encountered Lorenzo for the first time.

Machado had just returned from his new job. When he came into the kitchen, he discovered O'Hanlon having coffee with Luisa and talking earnestly. Luisa introduced the two men. Machado was polite but distant to O'Hanlon. He moved past the little man, and was on his way to the hall bathroom to wash up before dinner when O'Hanlon said:

"Mr. Machado, I'd like to talk to you about Teddy, if I may."

Lorenzo stopped, turned and regarded O'Hanlon with a glacial stare.

"You are a guest in my house, Mr. O'Hanlon," Lorenzo said evenly, "so I will not be rude to you. But Teddy is my son. His upbringing, his problems, what is good and bad, is of no concern to you. Understood? None of this would have happened, but he wears that idiotic outfit and wants to play cowboys. Of course that gang beat him up. . . ."

"Being a guest in your house, I don't want to be rude, either," said O'Hanlon in flawless Spanish. "But in all due respect, *Señor* Machado, you are full of shit."

The little man had spoken so softly and in Spanish, that Lorenzo wasn't certain he had heard O'Hanlon correctly. O'Hanlon properly interpreted Lorenzo's puzzled look.

"You heard me right," said O'Hanlon in English. "You don't know what the hell yer talkin' about. And I don't care if I never see you again, Machado, but yer gonna hear me out!"

Machado gazed at the wiry little man in wonder. Lorenzo had seen many cockfights, and O'Hanlon reminded him of nothing more than one of those ferocious birds. The little Irishman was almost dancing from foot to foot with an anger that seemed barely controlled. Still, O'Hanlon did not raise his voice.

Despite the disparity in their physical sizes, something within wisely counseled Lorenzo to listen. It was just as well, for he didn't realize how close he was to serious harm at O'Hanlon's hands. Lorenzo shrugged expressively and said, "Very well. I've had a long day, and I must wash up before dinner. I will speak to you in my living room. You will wait for me there."

When Lorenzo, washed and wearing a clean shirt, returned to the living room, O'Hanlon was standing, gazing out the window. Machado had removed his grease-stained work shoes and padded silently into the room. Although the little man had his back turned, and could not possibly have heard Lorenzo come into the room, he turned the instant Lorenzo entered. Machado waved O'Hanlon toward a chair, but the smaller man declined with an impatient shake of his head.

"What I got to say won't take long," O'Hanlon began. "I don't haveta sit down."

He left the window and approached Machado with a sinuous, eerily silent gait. "Now lissen, Machado," he said. "Do you wanna know why those punks beat up on yer kid? It wasn't because of the way he was dressed. It was because yer kid works for me it happened."

"Just what I've been saying. . . ." Lorenzo began, then seeing the look on O'Hanlon's face, he trailed off into silence.

"Those creeps were part of The Avengers," O'Hanlon continued. "And for yer information, Machado, they're the rottenest, creepiest bunch in this part of town. They got knives, and they got guns, too. When they seen Teddy goin' by every day, and found out where the kid was workin', they ganged up on him. They wanted him to steal ammo from my store. For their handguns!"

"I didn't know. . . ."

"Damn right, yuh didn't know," snapped O'Hanlon. "Yer so full of yer own ideas, and yuh never talk to the kid! Yeah, I know about that, too," O'Hanlon said, noting Machado's expression. "And it's too damned bad you don't talk to him. On account of that is one fine kid you got there. He took that beatin' because he wouldn't play ball with The Avengers."

"It wouldn't have hap—"

"I don't want to hear that crap!" said O'Hanlon. "Your attitude sucks, y'know that? The first time I met that kid of yours, he was puttin' hisself on the line, just trying to save a beautiful old Colt that you was tryin' to ruin. I figured out right then, that kid's got class. And now that I know him better, I'm sure of it. He must get it from his mother's side of the family. He sure as hell don't get it from you! Goodbye, Machado!"

Before Lorenzo could utter a word in reply, O'Hanlon had turned, and with a graceful catlike stride, left Lorenzo alone in the living room.

Machado noted that O'Hanlon opened and closed the front door as silently as he had walked. One moment he was there in the foyer archway. In the next, Lorenzo saw him appear at the curb where his venerable Chevrolet panel truck was parked. Silently, he got in on the driver's side. The engine started with a silky rumble that belied the miles it had covered in 16 years. Lorenzo couldn't suppress a slight shudder, though he knew no reason for it.

The next two weeks saw a marked increase in activity at the emergency room of Inglewood General Hospital. Members of The Avengers were admitted every night, all of them seriously injured. Juvenile authorities were puzzled. The social workers assigned to The Avengers knew that there had been no recent gang wars. Yet, some group of persons unknown was inflicting terrible injuries upon The Avenger's highest leaders.

Even the nature of the wounds was a mystery, for these were not the routine gunshot and stabbings common among the ranks of The Avengers. Neither the emergency room staff nor the Juvenile authorities received any explanation for these strange hurts. None was expected; the code of the barrio demanded silence.

But how had these grievous injuries been inflicted? Separated shoulders, broken arms and legs, ruptured abdominal walls, rib cages caved in like broken toys, and all with no sign of any weapon having been used! The idea that such horrendous damage could have been done by bare, callused, knobby-knuckled hands would have been instantly dismissed, had anyone thought of it.

The spate of mayhem among the leaders of The Avengers had one other unexpected, salutary effect. With the bulk of The Avenger's leaders hospitalized, the neighborhood enjoyed a period of relative freedom from street crime and forcible entries. After a few more days, the mysterious injuries ceased, leaving the puzzle forever unsolved.

Fourteen

I can't go to the exhibition match this weekend, Al," Teddy said.

"Just because you don't have the clothes to wear?" said Al Molina. "That's foolish, Tiger. It's how good you shoot, not what you wear that counts."

"Well, you got a swell outfit," Teddy protested. "And all the shooters that day at Knott's were wearing neat clothes, too. That ain't the worst part, either. My boots don't fit me anymore. I ain't even got a hat! When those creeps worked me over, they threw my hat down the sewer."

"The kid's right, Al," put in Tom O'Hanlon. "Who ever heard of a gunslinger wearin' sneakers?"

"Well, I could loan you some more coins, Tiger. . .," began The Champion.

"No, Al," Teddy said quickly. "You've already done so much for me the way it is. You been teaching me for six months, you got me that swell Fast Draw pistol and rig . . . ."

"And you paid me back every dime. No, I don't mind, Tiger."

"But *I* do," said Teddy firmly. "A pistol and a rig, that's different. But clothes, that's my end. Don't you see?"

"I respect your pride, Tiger," said Al Molina. "But you shouldn't worry about what you wear. Fast Draw people aren't snobs. They come from all walks of life. There's a few millionaires, real ones, that are into Fast Draw. And you'd never know it to look at them. One of them shoots in bib overalls! There isn't a man or woman I know of in Fast Draw who'd put you down for what you are, where you come from, or how you're dressed. In fact, after the shooting part, that's the best thing about Fast Draw. We're all equals, and it's how good you shoot that counts."

"I hear you, Champ," said Teddy. "But you see, there's . . . somebody coming out to see me shoot."

"Hey!" said O'Hanlon. "You mean yer old man is loosening up? Yer folks are comin' out?"

"No, Tee," Teddy replied. "We still ain't talkin'. He's as salty as ever. But I'm eating meals at the table with him again. That's since I got knocked around. But he'd never go to a shoot. I wouldn't ask him. I can't. We ain't talking."

"Then who are yuh worried about seein' yuh? If . . ." O'Hanlon's face took on an expression of malicious glee. "A dame!" he crowed. "It's gotta be a dame! How long is this been goin' on?"

"About a month," Teddy admitted, smiling sheepishly. "She's really neat, Tee. She likes western movies and . . ."

Teddy began to explain his feelings for Linda Perez. Actually, no one had been more surprised by the growing relationship than Teddy himself. Always uncomfortable in the presence of girls, Teddy found himself remarkably at ease with Linda. There was none of the banter and putdowns so much a part of boy-girl conversations in the New York barrios when he spoke with Linda. In fact, there was little talk that didn't originate with Teddy.

It had begun when, timidly, Teddy had invited Linda to a movie at a neighborhood theater. A revival double bill of *Shane* and *Whispering Smith* was being offered as part of an Alan Ladd film festival. Teddy and Linda had gone dutch treat and shared popcorn and soft drinks, each with eyes riveted to the screen. Never had Teddy met a girl so taken with the Old West!

Walking home, Teddy had repeated to Linda many of the comments about movie cowboys he had heard so often from Benito Machado. Linda received each bit of information as though Teddy himself had thought of it. The girl's open admiration for Teddy's opinions caused Teddy to walk taller as they approached Linda's house. Teddy noted that although the porch light was on in front of the small house, the rest of the house was in darkness.

"Gee, Linda," Teddy had said. "I think your folks are asleep already."

"No, my mom is at work," said Linda, leading Teddy up to the porch. "We won't disturb anyone if you want to come in."

"What about your dad?" Teddy asked. A sad look crossed Linda's face.

"My dad died six years ago," Linda replied softly. "When we

used to live in Arizona. We had a little *rancho* there. I don't remember Daddy too clear anymore. Just him riding on his horse and me riding in front of him, holding onto the saddle pommel. I . . ." Linda stopped as she saw the way in which Teddy was looking at her. "Did I say something wrong, Teddy?" she asked.

"No. Not at all," said Teddy in amazement. "You tellin' me your dad was a real cowboy? He owned a ranch, and all?"

"Not a ranch, exactly," Linda replied. "It was more like a farm. But we did have horses and cattle. We had about 20 head of whiteface."

"I feel like a fool," Teddy said quietly. "There I was telling you about where it's really at with cowboys. And you used to live on a real rancho. I musta handed you a laugh," he concluded bitterly.

"Oh, please don't be hurt!" cried Linda Perez. "I didn't mean to hurt you Teddy. Honest! I'd like to cut out my tongue for what I—"

Linda broke off speaking. Then suddenly, before Teddy realized what was happening, she grabbed the boy in a two-armed embrace and kissed him soundly. Completely flabbergasted, Teddy stood and received his first kiss from someone outside his family. As Teddy remained unmoving, in a state of near-shock, Linda opened her front door and disappeared inside of the house.

Teddy stood on the porch, looking at the door. A split second later, it opened again and Linda stuck her head out of the doorway momentarily.

"I . . . think I love you, Teddy," she said, and promptly disappeared.

Try as he might, Teddy was unable to remember walking home. And since that time, the only thoughts in Teddy's mind exclusive of his Fast Draw practice, had been of Linda Perez.

"Spare me the details," laughed O'Hanlon. "I'm sure she's the greatest thing since sliced bread. And beyooootiful, too."

"She is. She is!" Teddy began, then stopped. He looked at Al Molina and Tom O'Hanlon, who were both grinning from ear to ear. Teddy turned deep red and fell silent. "Ah the hell with you guys," he said. "You're makin' fun of me."

"No we ain't, kid," said O'Hanlon. "Just ribbin' yuh a little, is all."

"But this girlfriend of yours may explain why your shooting time has been off for the past month," said Al Molina. "You were shooting better before. A month back, in fact.

"You aren't concentrating hard enough, Teddy. It's like I was saying before. Concentration is everything. It's not the suit, the boots or the hat. Those are all trimmings. You can't be daydreaming up there on the firing line, Tiger. There's got to be only one thing on your mind: your move when the light flashes. And if you've practiced right, you won't have to think about the move, it'll come naturally. But you must concentrate. Come on, Tiger. Let's fire a few more rounds."

The Champion reloaded, and side by side with the boy, fired another five rounds. "Good time!" called O'Hanlon on the last round. "I seen you watched yer breathin' that time, kid."

"Breathin'?" queried Al Molina, mimicking O'Hanlon's accent.

"Yeah, breathin'," repeated O'Hanlon. "That's somethin' you wouldn't listen to me about. I been showin' the kid how to breathe right under stress."

"Karate again, Tee?"

"Yeah. What's wrong with it?" said O'Hanlon belligerently. "You, Al. Yer a natural. You do everything right. It comes natural to you. You couldn't do nothin' wrong if yuh tried."

"Well thanks, Tee, for the kind words."

O'Hanlon made a pushing-away gesture. "But I'm talkin' about the rest of us regular humans. You're okay, but we need all the help we can get. An I'm tellin' yuh that karate works."

O'Hanlon pointed a finger at Teddy. "If I hadna showed the kid some karate, The Avengers could of maybe killed him. And he got in a coupla good shots before they ran all over him, didncha, kid?"

"I tried, Tee," Teddy admitted. "There was just too many of them."

"No shame in that, kid," said O'Hanlon. "But I bet they been leavin' yuh alone lately, ain't they?"

"Yeah, that's the funniest thing, Tee," Teddy allowed. "I can walk right past Philly's Soul on my way home now. And nobody bothers me. They don't even say a word."

"See?" said O'Hanlon smiling. "You just gotta teach 'em a little respect, that's all."

"Well, I'm glad about it, no matter why," said Teddy. "On account of I want to bring my Colt home tonight."

"You finished it, Tiger?" asked Al Molina. "Let me see!"

Teddy want into the front of the gun shop and returned with a large, purple velvet-lined glass case. In it lay Benito Machado's

Single-Action Army Colt. Its newly reblued finish gleamed as though the pistol had just come from the Colt factory. The man hours Teddy had lavished on refurbishing and mounting the Colt had more than paid off. The final touch was a handsomely engraved brass plate, set in the velvet background directly under the antique pistol. It read:

> **Colt Single-Action**
> **Caliber .45**
> **Property of**
> **Benito Machado**
> **1889-1979**

"Beautiful work, El Tigre," said Al Molina. "Just beautiful work!" And to O'Hanlon, he said: "Did you help with this, Tee?"

"Yououteryermind?" said O'Hanlon so quickly that his voice cracked. "The kid done it all! He even done the engraving with my tools. Only thing he didn't do was the glass and the velvet. He even got rid of the red velvet that came with the case, and got some purple someplace."

"Sorry, Tiger," said Al Molina. "It's just that you've been working for Tee for such a short time. The level of workmanship surprised me. Not only on the pistol, but on the case, as well. I congratulate you on a fine job," he said, extending his hand which Teddy took.

Teddy blushed deeply. Through the months he had known Al Molina, the highest words of praise he had heard from The Champion had been "Not bad time. Let's shoot again."

"He done such a great job because he's got the best teacher in L.A.," said O'Hanlon in due modesty. "The kid's gettin' real good. I been thinkin'. I could maybe take him on as a full apprentice when he turns 18."

Al Molina looked at Teddy with new respect. The Champion knew that O'Hanlon was not a man to say such things lightly. In fact, Molina had not gained his friendship with the little Irishman easily. It was a relationship that had to be worked at. Molina recalled how hard he had striven for praise from O'Hanlon in those early days.

Teddy, basking in the warmth of the compliments, felt his cup run over. Then, thinking of the exhibition match a few days off, the boy's face fell.

"What's wrong kid?" asked O'Hanlon.

"Nothing, Tee," Teddy lied.

"Yer thinkin' about yer girlfriend again, aincha?" O'Hanlon asked. Teddy nodded. "Well, don't worry," said O'Hanlon. "She ain't gonna love you any more or less if you wore a gunny sack to the shoot. And if she did, she ain't the classy lady you think she is."

O'Hanlon saw Teddy's look and hastened to add: "And she is, of course. No offense, kid."

It was time for Al Molina to leave. He gave Teddy a few more pointers on Fast Draw technique, then received assurances from the boy that he would attend the exhibition two days away.

"Don't worry, Al," said O'Hanlon. "I'll drive him out there."

"Now I *am* worried, Tee," smiled Molina. "I've ridden with you in that souped up truck of yours. It's a thrill a minute!"

"Ahhh, geddoutahere!" laughed O'Hanlon.

"I'm going, I'm going!" cried The Champion in mock fear.

After The Champion had left, Teddy and O'Hanlon cleaned up the back room and closed down the shop. Teddy tucked the display case, wrapped in brown paper, under his arm. He was about to walk out the front door when O'Hanlon said:

"Hold on, kid. I'll drive yuh home. I don't think you'll get any flack from The Avengers. But it don't pay to take chances with a gun that valuable."

O'Hanlon went to the curb and unlocked the passenger door of his Chevy panel truck. "I gotta put the truck away, anyhow," he said, opening the door. "Plenty o' room. Pile in, kid."

The truck's engine responded to the first crank of the starter with a muted growl. O'Hanlon worked clutch and gearshift and the truck smoothly pulled away toward Teddy's house. On the way, O'Hanlon asked:

"Aincha goona ask me, Teddy?"

"Ask you what, Tee?"

"If I'll drive yer girlfriend with us to Riverside on Sunday."

"Well . . . ."

"It's okay with me, kid. Just have her there on time when I come to pick yuh up, okay?"

"Gee, thanks, Tee!" Teddy said.

"Ahhh, shuddup," said O'Hanlon.

Fifteen

Lorenzo Machado was not a happy man. He had been unhappy for months. Since his confrontation with O'Hanlon, Lorenzo had come to regret deeply the stand he had taken. But what was he to do? Apologize to his own son? Unthinkable! A man who is the head of his household does not do such things, he thought.

And damn it all, I am right, Lorenzo thought! Guns are not things for any honest grown man to be fooling with, he reassured himself. And least of all, he added, a boy of 15. No, wait! Almost 16. Teddy would be 16 on January 5. Sixteen years old. Almost a grown man!

Where did the years go? Lorenzo asked. Machado fondly recalled the days back in New York when Teddy was small and before Benito Machado had come to live with the family. Teddy's birthdays were days of companionship with Lorenzo back then.

He smiled as he remembered telling a four-year-old Teddy that the whole Spanish-speaking world celebrated on the boy's birthday. It was true, too. Teddy's birthdate coincided with *El Día de los Tres Reyes*, the day on which Latino children traditionally receive their Christmas toys.

In those days, Lorenzo was to his son the wisest, bravest, most handsome man in the world. Today, he and his son were all but enemies.

Now the boy was in his room this Sunday morning in December. He was preparing to go out to Riverside, wherever that was. He would go there to shoot off his pistol with people, who unlike his father, shared the boy's interests.

Lorenzo had voiced no protest about Teddy going to the exhibition at Frontier World. In fact, he secretly wondered if it would have made any difference had he objected. It only would have gained him further animosity from his son, and worse, his wife. Luisa was a stranger to her husband of late. They shared a house and a bed, but no more than that. It had been so since the night Teddy was attacked.

Lorenzo was secretly grateful for the continuing affection of his daughters, but lately he had noticed a slight distance between himself and Iris. Perhaps it was the new school and her new friends, Lorenzo thought. That girl Linda Perez, he mused. It's as though she's moved in with us!

Nor did Lorenzo miss the looks that Linda Perez exchanged with Teddy whenever the two were together in his presence. By some strange coincidence, Linda Perez was always ringing the doorbell just a few minutes before Teddy was due home from work. And this did not distress Teddy at all, Lorenzo noted.

Were it not for the estrangement between Teddy and Lorenzo, the boy's father would have been delighted. This Perez child was a good girl. The sort one marries, Lorenzo thought fleetingly.

In his bedroom, Teddy stood up straight and tall, trying to see as much of his reflection as was possible in his mirror. But stretch and crane as he might, he was unable to see his feet. And he'd even tried standing on the bed!

Not being able to see his feet worried Teddy. For on his feet were a pair of Benito Machado's finest dress boots: black lizard skin. True, the toes were stuffed with toilet paper for a better fit. And yes, they did have a tendency to slide off his feet if he sat with his legs crossed. But by God, Teddy had a pair of dress boots to wear at the shoot!

He was wearing a western cut shirt in blue plaid and a pair of straight legged jeans he'd purchased at a discount store. Still standing before the mirror, he carefully tied a new bandana handkerchief about his neck. He noted a scratchy sensation and untied the scarf. He found a price tag staple he hadn't noticed. Teddy removed the offending scrap of metal and for the hundredth time, looked at his reflection.

Not bad, he thought. Not shabby at all. He scowled steely eyed at the image in the mirror. The cut under his eye had healed and left a finelined white scar on his cheek. It stood out in stark contrast to his olive complexion.

Luisa Machado had been heartbroken about the scar. It didn't bother Teddy, though. Not since Linda Perez told him that the scar made Teddy appear more macho, and somehow sinister.

In fact, Teddy rather liked the scar. It was like a decoration won in battle.

Teddy looked at Benito Machado's Colt in its display case, atop his bureau. Above it, on the wall, hung the old man's saber, setting off the framed yellowed photograph of Benito in uniform.

"I will make you proud today, bisabuelo," Teddy promised softly.

At that moment, the doorbell rang. By the time Teddy had dashed to the foyer, Lorenzo Machado had already opened the door to admit Linda Perez. She wore a deep brown western riding suit with a divided skirt. On her feet were cordovan colored boots.

She had a bright blue silk scarf at her throat, which accented the fairness of her complexion and brought out the bluish highlights in her glossy black hair. She was the most beautiful thing Teddy had ever hoped to see.

An uncomfortable silence fell on the group at the door. Teddy and Lorenzo were still not speaking. His eyes met Teddy's for a long few seconds. Happily, Linda Perez broke the hush.

"You look marvelous, Teddy!" she said. "Where did you get those swell boots? I really dig them!"

"My bisabuelo," Teddy replied. "He left them to me in his will."

Hearing Benito Machado mentioned was enough for Lorenzo. He turned and silently walked into the kitchen, where he found Luisa cleaning up after breakfast. As he entered the room, she suddenly became very busy with her work.

Lorenzo was about to sit down at the table, but changed his mind. He knew there would be no extra cups of coffee, small talk or endearments from his wife this day. He sighed inwardly and walked out the back door into the yard. A car horn honked from the driveway.

Lorenzo peered down the narrow passageway between his garage and the house next door. He saw the panel truck with the lettering O'Hanlon's Hardware Store on its side, and knew who the visitor was. He remained in the back yard, staring with unseeing eyes at the blighted avocado tree. No amount of work on Lorenzo's part had been able to make it bear fruit.

Lorenzo heard Teddy call to O'Hanlon from the porch. Machado had suspected correctly that O'Hanlon would not have come to the door. The little Irishman would not take a chance on seeing Lorenzo Machado. In a few minutes, he caught a glimpse of Luisa, walking with Linda Perez and Teddy to the curbside where the truck stood.

"You are so handsome, hijito," said Luisa to her son. "Almost a grown man!"

She gave the almost-grown man a hug that made Teddy take in his breath sharply. Then she stood back to admire Teddy once more. She laid a hand gently upon the cheek that bore the white scar.

"*Buena suerte, mi hijo*," she said softly. "I would go to this place and see you shoot. But that would be disrespectful to your father. You understand?"

"Sí, Mama," Teddy replied, and suddenly grabbed and kissed her.

Luisa stood unmoving as the truck pulled away. She put her hand to the cheek Teddy had kissed, then smiling, walked slowly back into the house.

Lorenzo remained in the yard. He heard the front door close as Luisa returned. He gazed at the back yard and the house in which he lived. He had a good house. He had a good job now. He had a good wife, and good children. Despite it all, he was desperately unhappy.

He wandered into the house and to the living room, where Luisa was seated on the couch, watching a Sunday morning evangelist show on the TV.

"Where are Iris and Alicia?" he asked.

"Church and Sunday School," replied Luisa, her eyes never leaving the TV set.

"When will they be back?" Lorenzo asked.

"Does it matter to you?" Luisa asked flatly. "They'll be back in an hour."

"It matters a great deal," Machado said, "because we have to drive a long time to get to Riverside and this Frontier place. If my son is bound to make a fool of himself in a public place, the least his father can do is be there!"

Luisa was out of her seat and into Lorenzo's arms before he had finished his sentence.

"We don't have to wait that long," she said excitedly. "We can pick the girls up after church. Missing one Sunday School class won't hurt them!"

"Then don't just stand around, woman," Machado said. "Get ready to go! I must locate this place on my road map!"

When Teddy first saw Frontier World, he couldn't believe it

was real. It was more than familiar. It was, brick for brick, plank for plank, the very town he had seen in scores of western movies. More than that, it was the exact town El Tigre guarded as marshal!

Save for the fact that if one looked past the low buildings, passing cars could be seen on the nearby San Bernardino Freeway, it was as though Teddy, Linda and O'Hanlon had entered a time machine and emerged in 1880!

The three walked down Main Street, the same unpaved street on which Teddy had fought so many battles as El Tigre. Past The Palace Hotel, The Long Branch Saloon and the General Emporium, they walked, with Teddy still round-eyed.

A grizzled old prospector walked by, leading a heavily laden burro. Teddy noted the hitching rails, the board sidewalks and false-fronted buildings. How many times had El Tigre walked this street, Teddy thought? And down there, right where Main Street ended . . . there was the horse-drawn, glass-sided hearse of Smiley, the Undertaker!

Looking completely a part of his surroundings, in a black broadcloth suit with a brocade vest, frill-front shirt and string tie, Al Molina came walking toward the small party. "Hey, El Tigre!" he called out, waving.

"Hi, Al!" Teddy called. And to Linda Perez, he said quietly, "That's the world's champion, honey. C'mon. I'll introduce you."

If Linda Perez was charmed by Al Molina, it was hard to discern. Outside of shaking hands with Al Molina, she did not leave Teddy's side, nor relinquish her grip on his arm. Teddy was secretly relieved. He had feared that if Linda Perez saw a *real* Fast Draw champion, that Teddy would look pale by comparison. And Al Molina on this day was every bit the world's champion.

Tom O'Hanlon's words about "classy ladies" came to Teddy's mind. Linda didn't know why Teddy gave her hand an extra little squeeze. Nor would it have mattered had she known. But Teddy had been a trifle concerned when Al Molina, on meeting Linda had said:

"El Tigre, you told me you had a best girl. But you never said how beautiful she is!"

Linda had only smiled and said, "That's all right, Mr. Molina. I don't tell all my friends how handsome Teddy is, either." Teddy had turned a deep maroon. It didn't help when O'Hanlon said to him, "Come on *handsome*, we gotta get set up at the firing line."

The foursome went to the reviewing stands and found good

seats for Linda and O'Hanlon. It was early, and the stands weren't crowded. Mostly, the people there were shooters, friends and family. After seating Linda and O'Hanlon, Al Molina said to Teddy, "Come over to my car. I got something I want to show you." The boy accompanied Al Molina to the parking lot.

The Champion opened the trunk of his car and took out a large, lightweight box, which he handed to Teddy. "Now I don't want to hear any 'I-owe-you-this, you-owe-me-that' crap," Molina said firmly. "This is a gift from me to you. Friend-to-friend, *entiendes*? Now, open the box, Tiger," he said, as Teddy tore open the parcel.

It was a black Stetson hat with a domed crown and a straight brim. Teddy lifted it gently, almost reverently from its box. If The Champion noticed Teddy's eyes fill with tears of joy, Molina made no comment.

"Hope it's the right size, Tiger," The Champ said. "I had to guess at it."

"It's perfect, just perfect, Al," said Teddy setting the hat squarely upon his head.

"Great boots you got, too," said Molina. "Snakeskin?"

"No, lizard," Teddy replied. "They're my bisabuelo's. They really don't fit, though. I got toilet paper stuffed in 'em. In the toes."

"I won't tell if you don't," laughed Al Molina. "You know, the first time I went to a shoot, I didn't have a hat of my own. I wore my dad's. It didn't fit, and I had to stuff the inside of the sweat band with toilet paper! Isn't that something? We both used the same thing to get our outfits together!"

"Honest?" Teddy asked. "You ain't sayin' that to make me feel better?"

"I swear it, Tiger," said Molina holding up his right hand. "In fact, it was appropriate that I used toilet paper. On my first shoot, I went straight down the toilet. I couldn't have hit the floor if I fell out of bed!

"*You*, Al?" said Teddy in wonder. "I can't believe that."

"You better," Molina said. "I made a poor showing that day. I was too nervous. I couldn't concentrate. It was on that day I found out what it was like to shoot with the whole world watching.

"Up to then, I had only fired in my dad's garage. I tell you, El Tigre, it's a whole other ball game when they're watching you."

Molina saw the look on Teddy's face and said, "Look, El Tigre, I didn't say this to put you up tight about your first shoot. I just don't want you to think you're gonna be the greatest your first time out. Just remember all you've learned. And don't think about anything else. And I mean *anything*!"

"I'll try, Al. I'll really try."

"Good man!" said Molina clapping Teddy on the back. "You can't do more than that! But let's get back to the stands. My father is here today. You never met him."

When Teddy and The Champion returned to the reviewing stands, the targets and balloons were already set up. A man wearing a shirt that read Compadres Gun Club across the back was checking the timing equipment. As they neared where he was working, Al Molina called out:

"Hey, Papa!"

When the man turned, Teddy saw that he looked more like The Champion's older brother than a parent. Al introduced him to Teddy.

"Dad's going to be the timer and announcer today, Tiger," said Al Molina, Jr.

"That's right," said the elder Molina. "How do you want to be introduced, Teddy?" Then seeing the boy's blank look, he said, "I mean when you come up to the firing line, boy. I introduce you to the audience— say your name and where you're from, you know?"

"Teddy goes by El Tigre," said The Champion.

"Just El Tigre?" asked Molina senior. "No last name?"

"Just El Tigre will be fine," said Teddy in his deepest voice.

"Okay, Tiger," said the older man, smiling. Teddy noticed that when he smiled he looked just like The Champ.

Molina turned to his son and said, "Berto, let's go over in the stands and talk with your strange friend, O'Hanlon. He's been bending my ear about El Tigre here for the past 15 minutes."

They began walking to the grandstand. "By the way, El Tigre," said Al senior, "I met your girl. She's beautiful. Reminds me of 'Berto's mom when she was young."

"I will never find this place!" moaned Lorenzo Machado. "This entire state of California is one huge freeway with no damned exits!" Luisa said nothing, and quieted Alicia as well. The Pontiac sped on, toward Riverside and Frontier World.

"Our sixth shooter of the day is new to most of you," said Al Molina, Sr., over the public address system. "He prefers to be known as El Tigre."

There was a slight spatter of applause from the stands. Teddy risked a quick glance and saw that it came from where O'Hanlon and Linda Perez were seated. Trying to bear in mind all he had learned about Fast Draw and the breathing lessons from O'Hanlon, Teddy walked nervously up to the firing line. Al Molina, Jr., waited there to load Teddy's pistol.

"Loading for El Tigre is the World's Champion Fast Draw, Men's Division," announced Al senior over the horn.

"We know who he is, Al!" called a heckler from the stands. "But who's the mystery shooter?"

Teddy felt the blood rush to his face at the remark about his *nom de guerre*. But The Champion had Teddy's pistol loaded and ready. He handed it to Teddy and said: "Don't let the remarks get to you, Tiger. The stands are full of shooters today. They're unmerciful kidders, all of them. You just take care of business up here, okay?"

Teddy made a few practice draws once Al junior stepped back. He immediately heard a remark from the stands. "Molina's style. I think we got a ringer here, today."

The remark didn't fluster Teddy. He was flattered. He nodded to the timing table.

"Ready on the firing line! . . . Shooter set!" called Al senior.

* * * * * *

El Tigre stood eight feet away from Ike Clanton. He could see the black, unshaven stubble on the big man's cheeks. He saw a bead of perspiration start at the big man's brow and trickle down his face. Cool as ice, El Tigre said, "Anytime you're ready, Clanton . . . ."

The outlaw went for his gun! El Tigre's pistol spoke its deadly message . . . .

* * * * * *

"Time: 80.05!" called Al Molina, Sr.

The Champ came back to the firing line. "Terrible time, Tiger," he whispered. "What's wrong?"

"I dunno. Nerves I guess."

"Try to settle down," counseled The Champion and left the firing line. Teddy again faced the target, a single balloon eight feet away.

"Shooter set!" called the announcer . . . .

* * * * * *

El Tigre smiled thinly. Clanton's shot had gone wild. The marshal had seen that the big man's draw was off the line when he made his move. He had used his own shot only to shoot Clanton's hat off. Clanton was frozen with fear now, his gun still in his hand.

"Try again, Clanton," growled El Tigre . . . .

* * * * * *

"Miss!" called Al senior over the mike. Teddy blinked at the unburst balloon inside the metal target ring. The strobe light above it was still flashing as though in derision. A mocking voice called from the stands.

"Some Tiger! Or is that a pussycat?"

"Let's hold down the chatter in the stands!" called The Champ's father. "Shooter set!"

The Champion hadn't said a word to Teddy after the embarrassment of an outright miss. Teddy wished fervently that the ground could open up and swallow him whole. Suddenly, the light flashed!

This time, Teddy didn't think about his move. It was as though the pistol magically appeared in his hand. His left hand swept across his body, moving the hammer of the pistol to cocked position as his finger lightly stroked the hair trigger. Before Teddy knew what had happened, it was all over!

"Time: 40.02" called Al Molina, Sr.

"That's it. That's it!" whispered The Champion from behind him. "You did everything right that time. Good shooting!" In that moment, Teddy grew a foot in stature.

"Final round," called Al senior. "Shooter set!"

* * * * * *

Clanton's gang was ready. Main Street in Dodge was bare as a pauper's dog's bone, save for the unshaven men with guns who awaited a chance at El Tigre. Safe behind their walls, the townspeople peered timidly through windows at the drama unfolding on the dusty street.

El Tigre caught a hint of motion from an alley. He whirled and fired . . . .

* * * * * *

"Miss!" cried Al Molina, Sr. Teddy stood numbly as The Champion's father read off the boy's average shooting times.

To make his misery complete, Teddy had been outshot by the only other novice shooter of the day. And that shooter had been a 14-year-old girl! Al junior said nothing when Teddy returned to the stands where Linda Perez awaited.

"You were great!" was the first thing Linda said when Teddy returned.

It nearly brought tears to Teddy's eyes. He knew he hadn't been great. He had been just rotten. If the boy had known how to drive O'Hanlon's truck, he would have run to it and fled. He knew that his face was red.

He avoided O'Hanlon's eyes as he said to Linda, "I was awful . . . It went all wrong . . . I . . . ."

"Shuddup," said O'Hanlon quietly. "It's done. It's over. All you should be thinkin' about is the next event. That's the double balloons."

"But I couldn't even hit *one*!" Teddy protested.

Teddy felt a hand on his shoulder. He looked up to see The Champion's father standing by his side. Teddy had been the last shooter in the single-balloon event. Finished for the moment with his timer's duties, Al senior was taking a break.

"El Tigre," said Al senior. "Can we talk someplace? I mean, if that's all right with you and your friends?"

Linda and O'Hanlon nodded assent, and The Champion's father and Teddy strolled down the unpaved street together. As they did, Teddy felt a sinking sensation in the pit of his stomach. For coming down the Main Street of Frontier World, and headed straight for them, were Luisa Machado and Teddy's two sisters. To Teddy's intense dismay, they were accompanied by Lorenzo!

Teddy wanted to bolt. He quietly blessed Al Molina, Sr., when the older man led him to an untraveled alley alongside the General Store and Emporium. Teddy hoped with all his heart that his family hadn't seen him.

"I watched you on the firing line, El Tigre," began Al Molina, Sr., "and I think I know what's wrong." Teddy remembered in a flash that his hero, The Champion, had been taught by this man.

"Is it my move that's wrong?" he asked quickly. "I been practicing like crazy. I don't know what went wrong. I might have—"

"Billy the Kid," said Al Molina, Sr., cryptically.

"Huh?" said Teddy.

"Billy the Kid, I said," replied Molina. "That's who I used to shoot it out with. You *are* shooting at an imaginary foe, aren't you?"

"Yeah!" Teddy replied in wonder. "How did you know?"

"I didn't, for sure," said Molina. "I guessed. But I think that everyone starts out that way. Shooting at some imaginary opponent. I'm surprised that 'Berto didn't warn you about that.

"Or maybe I'm not surprised. 'Berto himself was terrible that way. With him, it was always Jack Palance, like he was in *Shane*. Maybe my son was ashamed to admit it. It does seem childish. Like a kid playing make-believe cowboys."

Teddy hoped that the shadow of his Stetson brim hid his look of embarrassment. "You're right, Mr. Molina," Teddy admitted. "I was shooting at Ike Clanton."

"What is done is done, El Tigre," said Molina, smiling. "So you must think of this! Your real opponent up there on the firing line is not an outlaw. Your opponent is yourself, Tiger. You must conquer your nervousness. You must allow no daydreams to distract you. Once you you hear me call 'Shooter set,' it should be the last thing you hear until your shot is over. There is no one shooting against you, son. Not even the other contestants. There can be no emotions involved, only the target, the light and you."

"I'll try to remember, sir," Teddy said earnestly.

"Don't try, do it!" said Molina senior firmly. "I have watched you, El Tigre. You have learned your lessons well. In fact, when my son 'Berto was your age, he didn't do everything near-perfect as you did that time."

"Honest?" said Teddy, his eyes wide. "I was really as good as Al? At his age, I mean?"

"Better," said Molina senior, smiling. "Now, I am going back to the grandstand. This time, I will not officiate. I want to watch you without distractions. Vandenburg can take over for me. Go back to the stands and that pretty girl of yours. I want to circulate among the crowd and boast about my son."

"Really?" Teddy asked.

"Really," laughed Molina senior. "Alberto won't brag. It's unmanly. But his proud Papa can boast. And does." He clapped Teddy on the shoulder. "Now go back to your girl before some slicker tries to take her from you."

Had his oversized boots fit him better, Teddy would have run back to the stands. But first, he peered carefully around the corner of the alley. Teddy didn't want to run into Lorenzo Machado. A thousand questions buzzed in his head about seeing his family present at the shoot. Especially his father!

But bearing in mind Al senior's injunction against distractions, Teddy wanted no breaks in concentration attributable to family problems. Seeing the street was clear, Teddy walked to the grandstands as fast as his boots and gunbelt would allow. Teddy was so intent on watching the stands that he walked directly past Lorenzo Machado who stood in a doorway, some distance from the audience.

Lorenzo almost reached out to touch his son as Teddy walked by. Somehow, he couldn't do it. He watched as Teddy rejoined Linda Perez and Tom O'Hanlon in the stands. They were joined by Luisa and the girls. Lorenzo saw the joy in Teddy's face when Luisa greeted him. There would be no joy were I with them, he thought.

Lorenzo surveyed the scene from where he stood. There were about 75 spectators in the grandstand seats. Almost all the men were dressed in elaborate western garb, their outfits all flashier than anything Teddy had ever worn to Lorenzo's mortification.

And these were grown men! Lorenzo marveled. It was Lorenzo's second surprise since arriving at Frontier World. The first had come in the parking lot. It had been filled with expensive automobiles, most of them bearing decals identifying their owners as members of various Fast Draw clubs. There were Mercedes-Benzes, a number of other marques that Lorenzo couldn't readily identify, and one shining bright Rolls-Royce convertible.

Lorenzo had been near intimidated until he parked alongside a battered 1965 Chevrolet that also bore a gun club sticker. Machado was lost in thought when a youngish man came up to him and said:

"Excuse me, but are you Mr. Machado?"

"Yes, I am," said Lorenzo. "Can I be of some help to you?"

"I am Al Molina," said the youngish man. "My son is the World's Champion Fast Draw."

Lorenzo shook the proffered hand of Al Molina, Sr., and replied:

"*Mucho gusto*. My son is—"

"Pretty damn good as a shooter," said Molina, finishing Lorenzo's sentence. "You should have seen him shoot earlier today."

"He did well, eh?" said Lorenzo, noncommittally.

"I have told your son that he is a better shooter at his age than my son, The Champion, was."

"He is?" queried Machado, openly surprised now.

"Now, don't rub it in, Señor Machado," admonished Molina. "I didn't come here to boast of your son's accomplishments. I came here to brag about my own son. If you want your son boasted about, you'll have to do it yourself."

"I wasn't asking for more praise for my son Señor," Machado said. "I was genuinely surprised. He has only been doing this . . ." Lorenzo searched for the term. He knew that Molina wouldn't take kindly toward Lorenzo referring to it as playing cowboys.

"Fast Draw," prompted Molina.

"This Fast Draw," Lorenzo continued, "for six months. That is a short time to become proficient at anything. He has done well, then."

"Very well, indeed," said Molina. "And tell me. Have you ever seen a competition before?"

"Once," Lorenzo admitted. "At Knott's Berry Farm. That's where my son first saw *your* son shoot. I too saw him."

"Marvelous, isn't he?" grinned Molina.

"One would suppose," Lorenzo replied. "I know very little about such things. My boy's bisabuelo was a real Wild West character. I think that's where Teddy got it from."

Lorenzo glanced over at the grandstand, where Teddy was talking with Luisa and his friends. "I must tell you, Señor Molina," Lorenzo said, "that Teddy has done all this without my approval. No, more than that. Against my wishes. I have never approved of guns for adults, let alone a growing boy."

"He's nearly a man, Señor," said Molina. "And I know much about him. From my son, and my son's curious friend, O'Hanlon."

Molina paused and looked Lorenzo directly in the eye. "Señor Machado, if you will permit me the liberty, I would say something about this family matter. I know that it is not for me to comment upon. *¿Pero, con permiso?*"

"Continue," said Lorenzo.

"Thank you," said Molina. "Let me tell you first about Alberto. A number of years back, I, too, was troubled about my son. But not for the same reasons you are troubled about Teddy. You see, Alberto was on the edge of going bad.

"In those days, I was not doing so well financially. We lived in the roughest part of East Los Angeles. There were gangs that terrorized the neighborhood. And any boy who did not belong to one of these gangs was fair prey for all of them. What was I to do? I couldn't move away. I couldn't afford it."

"This, I can understand," said Machado nodding. "It is this way in many parts of New York, as well."

"Bueno, you understand the problem," said Molina. "It was then, through a friend, I saw my first Fast Draw exhibition. My son was fascinated by it. I was too," said Molina smiling in remembrance.

"I suppose there's a little cowboy in all of us," he said. "In any event, I and my entire family took up this sport. The initial expense was steep, it's true. But much less than bailing my son out of a jail. Fast Draw became something that we did as a family. My wife, son, and I. Later, when she was old enough, my daughter joined us as well."

"Your daughter and wife?" asked Lorenzo in wonder.

"And why not the women as well?" asked Molina. "There is no danger in this sport. And *oígame*, Señor. While other men's sons were out cruising in cars and getting into heaven knows what, my son was at home with his family. We practiced in my garage.

"Alberto lost all desire to hang out with those hooligans. And today, he is a fine, honest, upstanding young man. He has made me very proud."

"I think I begin to see," Lorenzo said.

"I sincerely hope so," Molina said. "For Tom O'Hanlon has offered your son a rare opportunity. He will take Teddy on as an apprentice. To be a gunsmith is a fine trade. A profession, really. Teddy can make a fine living for the rest of his life with such training."

"This is so?" asked Lorenzo. "A good living?"

"Absolutely," said Molina firmly. "And O'Hanlon has told me his reason. He is impressed with Teddy's honesty, ambition and most of all, the boy's determination to *be* someone in this world. In this sense, you and Señora Machado are to be congratulated for raising such a fine boy."

Machado seemed to grow an inch taller at Al Molina, Sr.'s words. A smile that could not be denied spread across Lorenzo's swarthy features. Then he quickly set his face in a neutral expression.

"It's my wife . . . ." Lorenzo said haltingly. "She is a fine woman and strict Church. I can take no credit. I am busy each day working. Perhaps I should have—"

"Nonsense!" said Molina abruptly. "A boy learns to be a man by watching his father, no matter how busy the father may be! Your son couldn't be the fine young man he is without the example of two parents. But wait . . . the shooting is about to begin again. Let's go over closer. You *do* want to watch your son shoot, don't you?"

"You could not keep me away, Señor," said Lorenzo, smiling so hard that the skin stretched taut across his cheekbones. The two men walked together to the grandstands.

Just off the firing line, Teddy waited with Al junior at his side.

"Nervous, Tiger?" The Champion asked.

"A little," Teddy admitted.

"That's okay," The Champion said. "Make your nerves work for you. Concentrate, concentrate, concentrate!"

The Champion looked over at the timer's table. "They're about ready, El Tigre," he said. "Oh, by the way. Your folks are here. Do you still want to be announced as El Tigre?"

Teddy looked about him. He was "In the Hole," the next shooter on the line. He saw Luisa Machado in the stands, her eyes reflecting pride in her son. To his amazement, he saw Lorenzo, talking easily with Al Molina, Sr.!

Teddy especially noted the look of . . . well, what was it? . . . in the eyes of Linda Perez. She was looking at him the way Jean Arthur looked at Alan Ladd in *Shane*. Teddy hitched up his gunbelt and turned to The Champion, who still awaited his reply.

"No, not El Tigre," said Teddy firmly. "Tell them to say that I am Theodore Ramon Machado, of Inglewood."

"You got it, Teddy," said The Champion and went off to the timer's table.

"The next shooter will be Theodore Ramon Machado, of Inglewood," came the announcer's voice over the speakers. "Shooter on the line!"

Teddy walked up to the line, his very steps speaking determination. He took the loaded pistol from The Champion's extended hand. He nodded to the timer's table.

"Shooter set!" called the timer.

Teddy went into a light crouch, every fiber of his being concentrating on the task at hand . . . .

* * * * * *

El Tigre stood in the hot sun, watching Teddy stride up to the firing line. Belt and holster burnished to a high satiny finish and the sunlight glinting off the chrome of his pistol, the boy was every inch the pistolero. El Tigre smiled at the sight. He was no longer needed and he knew it. The great gunfighter turned and walked slowly up that same hot, dusty street that gunfighters have trod for a hundred years.

* * * * * *

Back on the firing line, Theodore Ramon Machado, fastest draw in all of Inglewood, stood ready. His hands were poised, waiting for the light to flash . . . .

THE END

Glossary

abuela *f.* grandmother
abuelo *m.* grandfather
además moreover, furthermore
"¿Ah, tú eres un latino, eh?"
   Oh, you're an Hispanic, eh?
¡Ay! Oh!

barrio Nueva York New York
   ghetto
béisbol baseball
Bien Well
"¡Bien hecho!" Well done!
bobo *m.* fool
"Buena suerte, mi hijo" Good
   luck, my son
Buenos días Good day

campesino *m.* farmer
Cerveza Schaefer local New
   York beer
chico *m.* little one (affectionate)
conchos ornaments
con dos huevos a real man
con mucho gusto with great
   pleasure

¡Díos mío! My God!

¿Entiendes? Do you understand?
   (familiar form)
Entiendo I understand
Entonces, dígame.
   **¿Precísamente lo que es
   que no entiendo?** Tell me
   then. Exactly what is it I don't
   understand?

finca *f.* farm

hijito *m.* son (familiar form)

katas Japanese word for the
   exercise in rhythm that
   Karate practitioners use as
   warmups

loco crazy

"¡Madre de Díos!" Mother of
   God!
"¡Mierda de perros!" dog
   droppings
"¡Mira!" Look!
muchacho *m.* boy
mucho much, many
mucho gusto pleased to meet
   you
mojón *m.* lump or clod
muñeca *f.* doll (term of
   endearment)

nom de guerre French phrase
   for "the name one fights
   under"

¡oigame! listen to me!
¡oye! listen!

pistolero *m.* gunfighter
"¡Precisamente!" Exactly!
Pues bien Very well
puta *f.* strumpet

querida *f.* darling
querido *m.* darling

un hombre muy macho a real
   man
un macho a real man (short form)
una quimera *f.* a dream